Fear of Missing Out

KATE McGOVERN

Farrar Straus Giroux ★ New York

Farrar Straus Giroux Books for Young Readers
An imprint of Macmillan Publishing Group, LLC
175 Fifth Avenue, New York, NY 10010

1   3   5   7   9   10   8   6   4   2

fiercereads.com

Library of Congress Cataloging-in-Publication Data

Names: McGovern, Kate, author.
Title: Fear of missing out / Kate McGovern.
Description: First edition. | New York : Farrar Straus Giroux, 2019. | Summary:
    Despite the loving intentions of her mother and boyfriend, sixteen-year-old Astrid
    wants to make the decisions about her life and death when her cancer returns,
    including exploring the possibility of cryopreservation.
Identifiers: LCCN 2018020372 | ISBN 9780374305475 (hardcover)
Subjects: | CYAC: Terminally ill—Fiction. | Cancer—Fiction. | Choice—Fiction. |
    Cryonics—Fiction.
Classification: LCC PZ7.1.M43524 Fe 2019 | DDC [Fic]—dc23
LC record available at https://lccn.loc.gov/2018020372

For Neheet

Any sufficiently advanced technology
is indistinguishable from magic.

—ARTHUR C. CLARKE

Fear of Missing Out

1.

I'VE ALWAYS THOUGHT AN ASTROCYTOMA
sounds like a shooting star. Right? Like something you'd want
to watch from the roof of your house or the top of a really tall
hill, probably lying on your back on a wool blanket and eating
popcorn. On the news, they'd be all like, "Don't miss the
astrocytoma shower tonight! It'll be most visible from nine to
midnight, weather permitting. Once in a lifetime!" You'd lie
there on your back on the blanket, waiting for it, and then it
would cross the sky over your head and you'd think, "That's
the *brightest, most beautiful* astrocytoma I've ever seen."

And it would be.

"Astrid. *Astrid.*"

I blink. There are tiny bursts of light swimming at the
corners of my vision. My astrocytoma.

An astrocytoma is not, in fact, a shooting star, though it

should be. It's a brain tumor, made of star-shaped cells. Astrocytes. Things of beauty, and instruments of death.

I blink again and my mother comes into view in front of me. She was sitting next to me a minute ago, and now she's hovering over me, her face too close to mine. "Astrid?"

Yes, my tumor matches my name.

"Yeah?"

"Did you hear Dr. Klein?"

My mother's face is splotchy. Her eyes are rimmed in red. I look from her to Dr. Klein, who's giving me her Serious Face.

"I'm sorry, guys," Dr. Klein says, clearing her throat. "I wish I had better news."

Poor Dr. Klein. I shouldn't be thinking about her feelings right now, but I am. Dr. Klein likes me. She already saved me once, when my brain first got tumored. Ninth grade. There was the surgery to remove it, and then the radiation, and then the chemo. It took nine months—my mother likes to say it took the same amount of time to start my life as it did to save it—and then everything looked good for a while. Like, doesn't-happen-that-often, almost-enough-to-make-you-believe-in-God good.

I don't believe in God, though. I believe in science, and there's a reason for that. Science is a kind of miraculous thing of its own, miraculous enough to make a star-shaped tumor go away for two years, which a lot of people said was impossible. But science is also reality, and it can only do what it can do. And now, according to the scan we're all staring at on Dr. Klein's computer screen, science has run up against its natural limitations.

That's my *brain* on the scan. My brain, the traffic control center of everything that makes me me. Just staring back at us in all its light and shadows. It never gets old, looking at a human brain.

Dr. Klein swallows. "Astrid, you know how to read this scan. I don't need to tell you what it says."

She's correct. The thing Dr. Klein did, besides saving me the first time, was make me love the brain—which, if you think about it, was pretty badass of her, considering that I had only recently come face-to-face with my own brain's potentially fatal flaws. She let me do an internship in her lab this past summer, and since my hair had mostly grown back by then, no one in the office knew I'd been one of her cancer kids just a year earlier. I was just a high school student with an interest in neuroscience, and she let me look under the microscope at slivers of normal and abnormal brain tissue, at scans just like this one, for patients with all kinds of astrocytomas and gliomas and medulloblastomas.

So she's right—I can read this scan. And it is not a good one. There's my brain, both hemispheres, and right there at the base of the brain stem, a foreign object of my body's own making: a jellyfish, a bubble floating away from a child's liquid-coated wand, a bright asteroid. A tumor made of stars.

"So where do we go from here?" Mom has her notebook out, the thick black one that's fraying at the corners, her keeping-track-of-Astrid's-cancer notebook. She clicks her ballpoint pen into action. My mother expects that there is always somewhere else to go from here.

I wait for Dr. Klein to break it to Mom: Do not pass go. Do not collect two hundred dollars. There is nowhere else from here.

"We can try more chemo, right?" Mom pushes.

"Yes, we can try a new drug combination. The options have improved somewhat in the last couple of years. There are no guarantees, but . . ." Dr. Klein hesitates. "There is one other thing that I think has some promise."

Not what I was expecting.

"There is a clinical trial launching in the spring, for an experimental immunotherapy that targets Astrid's particular type of tumor. You may be a good candidate for it."

I feel Mom's body physically lighten next to me, like she's about to levitate. "Okay," she says, her voice shooting up an octave like it does when she's excited. "Okay! We can do that. How do we get her into that? You can get her in, right?"

"I don't want to get your hopes up, guys. I need to be honest with you that this is . . . a long shot. At best. First we have to do more testing to make sure Astrid is in fact a candidate. Then she would have to be accepted—they'll look at a lot of factors to make sure she is healthy enough, relatively, to be part of the trial."

"So I have to be healthy enough to take part in a clinical trial for a cancer treatment?"

Dr. Klein cracks a smile. "I realize that's a tad ironic. But yes. That's why we'll do a chemo regimen regardless. Look, obviously, it's a trial. Some patients will receive the treatment; others will receive a placebo. We won't know which one Astrid receives, and we'll have no control over it."

"But if it works well, they'll cut off the trial and give the treatment to all the participants, right? They won't withhold it if it's working well?" Mom's talking fast now. She's read too much about all of this.

"They would, yes—but that's pretty uncommon, to be honest. The early results would have to indicate that we are *causing harm* to patients by giving them a placebo, that it is an ethical imperative to deliver the treatment to all the trial participants. It's a high bar."

Dr. Klein pauses. Mom is scribbling in her notebook, probably notes of things she wants to google when we get home, or even when we're stopped at a red light en route. (Some days I think I'm statistically more likely to die from my mother using her phone while driving than from cancer.)

"You should also know that the potential side effects from the trial could be intense."

"Chemo intense?" I ask.

"Potentially, yes, or more so, depending on how you respond. And there would be a good deal of time spent in-patient because of the frequent infusions. I don't say that to discourage you. I just think you should know the full picture there."

We're all silent for a moment. Mom's still jotting notes. I can feel her energy vibrating next to me. I've spent so much time in hospitals already. The idea of signing up for more—volunteering for it—makes me feel like the room is tilting.

Mom looks up from her notebook. "We can handle the side effects."

We? I love my mother. She'd do anything for me. But *we* do not have cancer.

Dr. Klein smiles gently. "Maxine, I want to be candid with you both. The trial has potential to lengthen Astrid's life. It may, or it may not. But it's unlikely to cure her completely. I'm really urging you not to pin all your hopes on this."

"Alison," my mother says in response, "you're telling me this is our best shot, right?"

Dr. Klein takes in my face, my relative reticence in this conversation. Then she looks back to Mom and nods. "That's where we're at now. I'd say so."

"Right," Mom says. "Can you really expect me not to pin my hopes on it?"

In the car, my mother takes deep, calming breaths in the driver's seat. I stare at the white of her knuckles, gripping the steering wheel as she drives.

"Astrid," Mom says, finally breaking the silence in our more-than-a-decade-old Honda. "It's okay. This is just a hiccup."

I knew the tumor was back well before we saw the scan

in Dr. Klein's office. There were the light bursts clouding my vision, for one. Then I started tripping again, losing my balance. And there were the headaches. A headache turning out to be a brain tumor is one of those crazy things that almost never happens. Like, when you get a really bad headache, you might think for a single, fleeting moment, "Man, this could be the big one." But it's pure hypochondria. It never actually happens in real life. Until it does.

I didn't tell my mother right away when it came back, because I knew she'd go all freaky maternal on me, and I wasn't ready to hurt her again. Maybe I wasn't ready to be sick again, either. So I lived with my tumor made of stars, just the two of us, for about a month. Until one morning, when the headache bloomed so hard and so fast that I puked all over myself, and fell on the way to the bathroom, and then I didn't have to say anything, because she knew as well as I did. I wish I could forget the look on her face when she came bursting out of her bedroom and found me on the hallway floor, covered in vomit. I stared up at her, my only participating parent, and me, her firstborn baby, and watched the panic come into her face like a cloud rolling in before a summer thunderstorm.

"I think this clinical trial has real promise. I mean, immunotherapy, right? That's what everyone's talking about." We stop at a light and, sure enough, Mom pulls out her phone and starts tapping away with one hand, the other still resting on the wheel.

"Mom, you're going to get a ticket."

"They can't ticket me unless they pull me over for some other reason."

"I think that's for not wearing a seat belt, Mom. I'm fairly certain they actually can pull you over for using your phone."

"I just don't want to forget what I'm . . ." The light changes. Mom drops her phone and we lurch into the intersection. "This could really work. I feel good about this."

I take my phone out and pull up Mohit's last text: *How'd it go?* it reads.

He doesn't need to ask. He knew, too, as soon as I told him the headaches were back.

I start to type a text in response: *Doomsday.* Then I delete it. I want to say something clever to Mo, to reassure him that I'm still *me*. But I can't. I close my eyes, press my head against the seat of the car. I'll call him when I get home. It will break my heart to break his heart all over again.

As we drive on, my mother keeps talking. About more chemo, more radiation, more trials, more, more, more.

"Mom. Please. Just stop."

She turns to me. "Babe, we still have time. We have options. You know that, right? We're not done here."

I run my tongue over my lips, which have gone very dry all of a sudden. I want to tell her that she's wrong. I *know* about clinical trials and new drug cocktails, I do. I know more than I should, thanks to my internship. Enough to be pretty much a shoo-in for the best neuroscience programs in the country for college, with Dr. Klein's recommendation, which is what I'd imagined I'd be doing after high school, right up until the headaches and the light bursts came back. I know that the chance of any kind of novel treatment working for me now, given everything, is about as close to zero as you can get without already being dead.

And more to the point, I know that sometimes—often—the treatment is worse than the cancer itself.

Instead of saying that, though, I nod. "Yeah, Mom. I know."

2.

I DON'T NEED TO CALL MOHIT WHEN WE GET
home, because he's waiting on the front steps when we pull
up. Mom idles the car and leans toward the window on my
side. "You go ahead. I'll find a spot." There's no parking lot for
our building, but Mom knows all the secret side-street spots
in the neighborhood. She claims she's mastered the art of VPS
(Visualizing the Parking Space), and then, *poof*, it appears.

Mo looks focused, and worried. He stands, taking his
scuffed saxophone case in one hand, and wraps his other arm
around me when I get to him.

"So?" he says as I fish my keys from my bag and let us into
the front vestibule. Junk mail and bills are poking out of our
mailbox, but I don't bother to collect them. We take the elevator to the second floor and slip into the apartment.

"Liam?" I call down the hall. I think my brother is still at
his friend's house, but I want to be sure. No answer.

Mohit closes my bedroom door behind us. "So?" he asks
for the second time. "What'd she say?"

I bury myself in his chest and wait until his arms are firmly wrapped around my shoulders to take a deep, exhausted breath. Then I pull my face away and look up at him. I shrug. "What we thought she'd say."

The confirmation of what we already knew ripples through him. I can see the muscles in his jaw tighten, and his eyes flicker away from my face and then back again.

"Shit," he says, finally. "Well. Now what?"

If you've read a lot of chick lit (or let's call it something less sexist and gross, like "lighthearted literature featuring quirky female protagonists and romantic plot lines"), and by the way I *have* read a lot of said literature—because, frankly, the better part of a year with cancer isn't the best time to catch up on your Dostoyevsky—you might imagine that Mohit would have a "crooked smile," whatever that means, and that his T-shirts would smell of fresh laundry, and so on. In fact, though, he has a perfectly even smile (when it's on display), with dimples as deep as tiny wells drilled in each cheek, and very nice teeth, and he never smells of fresh laundry because his parents buy the unscented, chemical-free, totally organic kind of detergent that doesn't smell like anything. The kind of detergent that costs twice as much as the regular store brand and that my mom used to splurge on, too, before she had, you know, brain surgeries to pay for. Kind of ironic, really, that as soon as I got sick Mom had to stop buying all the pricey natural products she'd hoped would keep us safe from getting sick in the first place. Now it's all chemicals and GMOs all the time around here. Doesn't seem to be making much difference one way or the other, as far as I can tell.

I shrug. "More chemo. And there's some trial in the spring. My mother has basically already signed me up for it."

Mo's face brightens, just like Mom's did in Dr. Klein's office.

"But I don't even know if I'm eligible yet. And even if I am, it's just so . . ." I trail off. I don't want to kill all his hope at once, but Mohit doesn't understand as well as I do just how slim a chance any clinical trial has of working in a meaningful way for any one patient. "Let's just . . . pretend it's not happening for a minute."

"This trial, or the tumor?"

"Both?"

He runs his fingers through my hair—my hair that practically just grew back, and now it'll be gone again—and then kisses me, and I close my eyes and exhale and let him pull me gently onto my bed.

Mohit and I met in ninth grade, BT (Before Tumor). It wasn't a magical first meeting—not particularly "auspicious," as Mo's father, who's a phlebotomist by day and officiates Hindu weddings on occasional weekends, might say. We were just in homeroom together. He'd moved from California for his mother's work, and he was all West Coast-y with kind of shaggy surfer hair. I'd never seen an Indian American kid with surfer hair, really, and I frankly didn't know they existed (which, I know, was stupid and/or a little bit racist of me). Anyway, I wasn't even particularly thinking about boys or boyfriends or anything remotely romantic. My best friend, Chloe, and I were really into this particular word game on our phones that was a super-trend at the moment, and that was what we were talking about in homeroom that morning when Mohit walked in and told Mr. McDowell that he'd just transferred and was he in the right room?

He was.

He sat down next to me, unfolded his schedule, offered me his hand for a shake, and introduced himself in a whisper. He pronounced his name clearly: *Mo-hit*. "You can say it, like, if Moe Szyslak from *The Simpsons* is playing baseball?" he said, as if he expected I'd need the help. "Moe hit the ball. Mohit." Then he asked if I knew where he was going for math.

I walked him there that morning, and all the rest of the mornings.

Four months later, a week after he'd first asked me if he could put his hand on my boob—over my shirt, obviously— and I'd said sure, I started noticing the headaches. And by spring, just when everyone at school was starting to think of us as one of Those Couples, Dr. Klein showed me a scan of my brain for the first time.

I hear Mom come in. There's a knock at my bedroom door.

"Mohit, are you staying for dinner?"

Mo looks at me and mouths, "Want me to?"

I nod. Mohit's presence at dinner will prevent Mom from talking too much about the clinical trial, and how she's *sure* I'll be eligible, and how she'll call the acupuncturist again and that'll help with the headaches in the meantime, and how I should really put on my Optimism Pants. Except she'll be completely, obviously, gripped by fear. She thinks I can't tell, but . . . come on.

"Sure, thanks, Maxine!" Mohit calls toward the door.

I listen to hear if Mom's retreating down the hall or hovering. After a moment, footsteps pad lightly back toward the living room.

Mohit rolls over, throwing a leg across mine. "How's your head?"

"Um, well, it doesn't feel like an eighteen-wheeler is driving back and forth over my brain stem at the moment, so that's an improvement. My vision's . . ." I look toward the ceiling, watching those circles of light dance around the room. I'm trying to think of the words to describe the blurring around the edges, the bright flashes, the dreamlike quality of what I see in front of me right now. "Kind of psychedelic. Some people would pay good money for this."

Mohit sighs. "Why do you do that, Astrid?" He flops on his back, one hand draped across my chest.

"Do what?"

"That thing. The minimizing thing. You can just tell me when you're in pain. I can deal."

I resist the urge to roll my eyes, because Mo hates it when

I do that and I'm not looking to pick a fight right now. But this is not the first time we've had this conversation.

"I'm not minimizing. I'm just . . ." I pause. It doesn't have anything to do with protecting Mohit; I *know* he can handle it. It's about me. I'm trying to retain half an ounce of my former self. The person I was BT. That's hard to explain, even to this person who knows me better than basically anyone.

"Remember what we were doing a minute ago?" I ask finally.

"What were we doing a minute ago?"

I flip over on top of Mo, straddling his waist with my legs, and press my whole body against his. I can feel his heart beating through his totally unscented, fair-trade, GMO-free sweatshirt, and my body rises and falls with the movement of his chest.

"Oh, is this what we were doing?" he asks. He slides a hand under the waistband of my jeans and rests it at the base of my spine. His hand on my bare skin makes me melt a little bit.

"Something like that," I say, running my hands up under his sweatshirt.

"Dude, your hands are like icicles right now!" he squeals, recoiling.

"I know they are, and your chest is very warm. Be nice to your cancer-ridden girlfriend."

He laughs. "So we're going there already, huh? You're a little bit cruel when you have a brain tumor, you know."

"Sorry. Can't help it."

We lie there for a few minutes, our breathing never quite in unison.

Eventually, Mo stretches an arm out from under me and takes the book from my bedside table. "Where are we going today?" he asks, flipping it around to look at the cover.

It's a Lonely Planet travel guide to Kenya.

"Kenya, huh? Anything good?"

"Safari in the Maasai Mara, but that's kind of cliché. Lamu seems like a must-see."

My used-travel-guide habit started the first time I got cancer. Someone had left one—*The Rough Guide to Japan*—in the chemo lounge and I started thumbing through it absent-mindedly, the way you do anything when you're in the middle of a chemo infusion. I'd never particularly wanted to go to Japan, but browsing through the descriptions of people-packed Tokyo and the Shinto shrines in Kyoto made the infusion go by more quickly. So I bought another one online—for Greece—and then another, and another, for far-flung islands and European hot spots and random parts of the United States, too. Places I'll probably never see in real life, and never knew I wanted to until I read about them. Traveling via guidebook isn't as good as the real thing, but it's better than nothing.

I take the book from his hands and put it aside. "Mo?"

"Astrid?" His dark eyes alight on my face expectantly.

I pause to think of how I want to say what I want to say. "I'm a little bit scared this time."

"Yeah," he says, so quiet I can barely hear him. "I'm a little bit scared, too."

Then I kiss him until my vision might be blurred from pleasure instead of pain and my lips swell and the weight is almost, almost, almost gone.

It's two in the morning when I wake up to pee. My head feels surprisingly clear, almost normal, and I roll over and run my hand over the Mohit-shaped wrinkles in the sheets next to me. He didn't really leave those wrinkles, of course; he left after dinner and a round of Wii bowling with Liam. But I can still feel him in the empty space next to me.

I tiptoe to the bathroom, careful of the creaky parts of the hallway. Outside Mom's door, I pause. There's muffled noise, like the TV is on. She must have passed out watching something, trying to dull herself into sleep with a late-night talk show or a PBS mystery on repeat.

The door is cracked slightly—ever since Dad left, Liam sometimes still likes to climb in bed with Mom in the middle of the night if he has a bad dream or something, even though he's eight now—so I nudge it open farther with my toe, careful not to make any noise, and peer in. I expect to see her asleep, tangled roughly in the blankets, with the blue glow of the television pulsing in the room. Instead, it's completely dark; the TV is off. And her body isn't limp like it would be in sleep. Even in the shadows of the room, I see her curled toward the opposite wall, in a fetal position under the covers, rocking back and forth. With every rock, she makes a low moan, almost a growl.

A floorboard groans under me and I freeze, watching Mom's shadow to see if it seems to register the noise. A moment later, she sniffles, rolls over, pulls the covers closer around her. She never turns toward the door, and I let my breath out slowly and step back into the hallway, toward the bathroom.

It feels like an impossible intrusion, like reading someone else's journal or checking their email, listening to my mother's private grief. The parts she doesn't want me to see. I have to shut it out before it sucks me in and I can't think about anything else.

3.

"TELL ME AGAIN WHY YOU THINK ANYONE AT this symposium knows more about my tumor than Dr. Klein?"

Mom pushes through the revolving door at the Expo Center. "Maybe they won't, Astrid," she says when we both come out the other side. "But Dr. Klein said even she was looking forward to checking out the most cutting-edge research in the field. So you never know, do you? Plus, the doctors leading the clinical trial will be here, and I don't think it would be a bad thing to make a personal connection with them."

I sigh. My mother has no idea that patients don't get into clinical trials by being friends with the research team. It's not like an AP class with the best teacher: you can't just talk your way in by bringing cookies to the guidance counselor.

Then again, it's true that Dr. Klein's comment about the cutting-edge research is the real reason I let my mother drag me along to this brain research symposium. I'm curious what they've got. But if Mom thinks I'm going to follow her around while she goes up to random researchers and pulls my scans out of their envelope, she's dreaming.

The symposium is supposed to be the biggest international conference of neuro-types anywhere. The lobby is teeming with science nerds weighed down with branded tote bags probably full of research papers, brochures, other people's business cards. In every direction, there are signs directing traffic toward the main exhibition hall, the bathrooms, the café, and others featuring the highlights of today's schedule. I grab a program, which is as thick as a phonebook for a small city, and flip through it. There's a long directory of all the exhibitors, plus a day-by-day schedule for the weekend. Today at one o'clock Dr. Klein is giving a talk on radical therapies for high-grade pediatric astrocytomas. I think I can skip that one.

"I'm going to do a lap," I tell Mom when we've registered and draped visitor badges around our necks.

Mom gives me one of her I-can't-with-you looks. "Fine, just don't leave without me, will you?"

"You have the car keys."

"You're really a pain in the ass, you know."

"You have only yourself to blame."

She smacks my arm with her program. "Meet me back here in an hour."

"You know, we have these crazy contraptions these days, they're called cellular telephones—"

"One hour, Astrid. Don't make me come looking for you."

"Roger that, Maxine."

Mom cocks one eyebrow at me. *"Maxine?"*

"It's just something I'm trying."

"Well, don't. One hour, Daughter."

"Yes, yes, *Mother*," I call over my shoulder as I wander toward the exhibition hall.

Inside the hall, I'm immediately overwhelmed by the chaos. Row after row of booths, all of them decorated in brightly branded tablecloths and trifold banners, stacked high with papers, books, baskets of souvenirs in the form of key chains and bottle openers and brain-shaped stress balls. My head throbs under the fluorescents. I take a stress ball from a table as I pass by, avoiding eye contact with the obviously twenty-something research assistant behind the table, and squeeze my fist around it as I wander down what appears to be aisle J.

I try to meditate on the squeezing as I walk, imagining that my brain is the stress ball and I'm massaging the pain out of it. Mom always tells me to try to visualize away my pain. Not in like a condescending way—she knows I need actual medication, obviously, like a lot of it sometimes—but she's a CNM (certified nurse midwife) when she's not in full-time Brain Tumor Management mode, and she's used to telling her own patients to breathe and focus and visualize things to manage their pain. Of course, I guess when your pain is temporary and in service of birthing a human, it may be more inclined to respond to mental pressure.

Anyway, my headache doesn't go away from squeezing the stress ball, but some of the anxiety brought on by the chaos around me seems to. Not that I have any kind of serious problems with crowds or anything, but with a few minutes of focused squeezing and deep breathing, I can already feel my heart rate slowing and the queasiness I recognize as nerves calming. Bonus of having a brain tumor and going through a crap ton of treatment for a year: I'm reasonably attuned to the signals my body gives me.

I pause to catch my breath at a table featuring research into a new blood test for variant Creutzfeldt-Jakob disease, one of those nasty human prion diseases that kills you slowly after taking away your motor skills, speech, and normal personality. Once again avoiding eye contact with a research assistant, I pull my phone out to text Mo while I perch against the edge of the table.

Then I pause and think better of it. I know he's going to ask if I've talked to the directors of the clinical trial; he can't help himself. Mohit is just like my mother, wanting to figure out the best course of action, the best *next steps*. He wants to feel like he's doing something other than watching me die. Which, let's be real—it's not like I'm terribly keen on croaking before I graduate high school either. And I guess I wouldn't want everyone around me to throw up their hands and be like, "Well, you're toast. Let's call Make-A-Wish and go to Harry Potter World." (Although I really, *really* want to go to Harry Potter World.) So I don't know what I want, exactly. But it feels like the positivity is forced, like we all have to rush toward optimism or the Angel of Death will somehow notice and take our despair as permanent defeat. Maybe I just want them all to give me a minute. With the despair part. A minute to feel really mad about this whole situation.

I text Chloe instead. She always lets me have a minute.

This place is a madhouse. Almost literally, considering the number of people with compromised neurological function probably roaming around. Present company included.

Clo writes back right away: *Questionable use of "literally," but I'll allow it on account of your brain tumor.*

My phone buzzes again. *Can we hang out later? It's book club night over here and I need to avoid All the Cambridge Ladies.*

I laugh. "Cambridge Ladies" is code for the abundance of uber-liberal white women in our neighborhood who wear tunics and leggings and make their own granola and drive used Subarus, among other common characteristics. Which basically describes our own mothers (minus, in my case, the Subaru).

Clearly, I type back. *I think Mo and I are doing a movie night. You in?*

She doesn't respond immediately, and I know she's probably momentarily pouting about spending another Saturday night with me *and* Mohit. It's not like Chloe hates Mo or anything. But she didn't take to sharing me all that well, especially at first. These days, she and Mohit have a kind of unspoken agreement that they put up with each other's constant presence in my life because what else are they going to do about it?

Finally, I see two dots appear on my screen while she types a reply. *I suppose I could third-wheel it yet again. For you.*

And don't tell me, the movie must be something that gets more than three stars. I know your weirdo boyfriend's weirdo Rule of Movies.

She's not wrong. Mo's Rule of Movies is that he never—*never*—watches anything that gets less than four point five stars on All the Rating Systems of the Internet. It's manageable, except when Chloe and I want to watch a really bad thriller with Liam Neeson and call it a day. Sometimes I just don't care if everyone else hated it because I am going to hate-watch bad Liam Neeson thrillers for as long as I've got left, and I am going to love them.

A voice comes over the loudspeaker announcing the start of the one o'clock presentations. I think of Dr. Klein, getting her PowerPoint deck ready so that she can show people my brain and tell them how the radical therapies fixed it for a year and then failed miserably. I'm sorry I let her down. I wish we'd waited another week to get the latest scans back. Then at least she could've made this presentation while I was still supposedly in remission.

I hang a left down aisle K, and a table catches my eye primarily because there's no one there. I mean, most of the tables have a few people at least hovering around them, perusing the literature or asking questions. This one is empty, except for a youngish guy behind the table, fiddling with the display.

I wander over. It's an exhibit for the American Institute for Cryonics Research, which I've never heard of. The guy seems far too young to have any kind of real job—he looks not that much older than me—but I don't see anyone else with him and he's wearing an exhibitor badge around his neck. He's trying to straighten one of the pop-up banners, and the top disengages from its frame and bounces back against his face.

"Dammit!" he says, under his breath.

"Want some help?" I ask, stepping in and grabbing one end of the banner.

"Thanks. Sorry. These banners are just . . . My boss doesn't understand the concept of 'get what you pay for,' know what I mean?"

I help him clip it back in the holder and straighten it out. Then I step away from the table.

"Thanks," he says again. "I'm Carl. Uh, sorry, Dr. Carl Vanderwalk. I'm still getting used to the 'doctor' part. I just graduated from med school. Anyway, Dr. Carl Vanderwalk, MD, PhD. Doctor, two ways." He laughs awkwardly.

I take his outstretched hand. "Astrid Ayeroff. Just a regular human."

"Lucky you—you won't end up drowning in debt like I am."

"Something like that," I say. I must look slightly distressed, because he furrows his brow and looks around.

"Water?" He passes me a bottle across the table.

"Thanks."

"So what brings you to the symposium?" he asks while I take a long swig of the water and try to visualize it moisturizing my brain and melting the headache away. It doesn't work.

I put the bottle down, half empty. "I love the brain."

He smiles. "It's a thing of beauty, isn't it?"

He's right about that. "Mmm-hmm. Thanks for the water, Dr. . . ." I've already forgotten his name, so I look at his badge more closely. "Dr. Vanderwalk."

"Please, just Carl. The doctor thing makes me feel old. They keep telling me I have to use it when I introduce myself because, I don't know, otherwise people think I'm like twelve or something and totally unqualified to talk about our work."

"Who's 'they'?" I ask.

"Oh, my boss. Here." He rummages around behind the table and pulls out a business card. "Dr. A. R. Fitzspelt. His first name is Argos, but don't tell him I told you that."

I take the card and drop it into my tote bag. "So what is cryonics, anyway?"

His face brightens, like he's suddenly been asked to rattle off a list of all the As he got in med school or something. "I'm glad you asked! Cryonics is the most advanced and exciting extension of cryopreservation. It's the science of body preservation. It's the future."

Images of industrial-strength freezers in a warehouse clouded with cold mist pop into my head. A team of mad scientists pore over glass caskets of freezer-burned bodies. I can almost smell the formaldehyde from here. For a moment, it feels like the room is spinning.

"I know what you're thinking," Carl says. "It sounds like science fiction."

"Something like that."

"I get that a lot. It's not, though, believe me. It's a legitimate choice more and more families are making for their loved ones at death, to preserve either their entire bodies or, in some cases, just their brains. Our facility is in Sedona, Arizona. It's the oldest cryonics lab in the nation. Our youngest client is just two years old. Our oldest is eighty-four."

I swallow, thinking of a two-year-old body engulfed in a deep freeze. "Preserve them to what end, though?"

"We're just beginning to explore the possibilities, of course," he says. "But the ultimate goal is to one day revive our patients."

I never say this, but I think the hair on the back of my neck is literally standing up. And for Chloe's sake, I mean "literal" in the dictionary-definition way this time.

He hands me a brochure. "You seem smart. Call us when you're looking for a job. I started as an intern. Now I'm the associate medical director."

My mouth has gone completely dry, and I suck down the rest of the water in one long swig. When I've finished, Dr. Carl Vanderwalk is staring at me quizzically.

"Are you okay?"

"I won't be looking for a job," I say. "I'm dying."

Before he can respond, I've walked away.

4.

PRECALCULUS IS NOT MADE FOR BRAIN TUMORS.

"So what do you have to know about your triangle, in order to use the law of sines?" Ms. Dahlmann scans the room for her next unsuspecting victim. I avoid eye contact. The numbers and symbols on the whiteboard at the front of the room—even from the front-row seat I had to take when my vision took its recent nosedive—are blurring.

"Come on, gang, you know this stuff." She keeps roving. "Mohit?"

Hearing Mo rustle in his seat, I turn around. He's at the desk directly behind me. I cock my head at him ever so slightly, challenging him to give Ms. Dahlmann what she wants. He gnaws on the end of his mechanical pencil.

"Well, you need two sides."

"And?"

He scrunches his face and stares at the board. "And . . . a corresponding angle?"

Ms. Dahlmann lights up. "Right, excellent. Or you could

have . . . what?" She moves on from Mo, and even with my eyes planted on my desktop, I can feel her staring at me. "Astrid? What else could you have and use the law of sines?"

I sigh and shift my eyes back up toward her. I feel suddenly exhausted, and resentful. My teachers know about my . . . brain. Against my wishes, Mom told the principal that the tumor is back, that my energy might be low and my vision is increasingly affected. Dahlmann was the one who suggested I move to the front of the room. I didn't want my teachers to know in the first place, since I'd prefer not to be branded as Cancer Girl all over again quite so soon. But if they *must* know, at least they could cut me some slack.

I shake my head. "Not sure," I mutter.

"Come on, Astrid. You've got this." Her voice is gentle, but she's not giving me an out. Dahlmann is very comfortable with uncomfortable silence in her classroom.

"Umm . . ." I stare at the board. It's not that I mind math, per se. I loved algebra, and precalculus is a lot of the same stuff, just more of it, like fancy algebra. But now I can barely muster the will to comprehend the equations and images staring me in the face. "I don't know, Ms. Dahlmann. Sorry."

Dahlmann looks at me for a moment more, as if she's trying to ascertain whether she should push me any harder, and then she moves on. "Sofia?"

Sofia Mayhew, who has hair so long she can sit on it, squirms at her desk. "I mean, I guess if you had two angles and a corresponding side . . ."

"Thank you! See that? Was that so bad, my friends? I didn't think so." She goes back to the board and starts sketching out an example problem of each type. I zone out, figuring since she's cold-called me once already, she's not likely to do it again.

On our way out the door after the bell, Dahlmann stops me. "Astrid. A minute, okay?"

Dahlmann's desk is sloppy with tests to be corrected and orphaned homework assignments. I try to focus my brain and eyes on her.

"Astrid," she says again, slowly. She watches the rest of the class empty out before continuing. When we're alone in the room, she clears her throat. "Look, I know you're struggling a little bit."

"I'm okay."

"I know, but . . . you're having trouble seeing. And you're having headaches again, right?"

She waits for me to answer. Finally, I give her a nod.

"Listen, I don't know what's next for you in terms of your . . . treatment."

It's obviously awkward for her to talk about this. I can't really blame her; it's awkward for everyone.

"But . . . I just want you to know that you can be honest with me about how you're feeling. Okay? If you're not up for class, I can give you some work to do in the library. But if you're here, I have to treat you like everyone else. You get that, right?"

I nod again.

"Okay. That's it."

"Thanks, Ms. Dahlmann." I start toward the door.

"And, Astrid."

Her eyes look a little watery. *Please*, don't let a teacher cry on me. Come on.

"I'm praying for you."

I swallow. "Thanks." I guess.

5.

WHEN I FIND CHLOE AFTER SCHOOL, SHE'S rummaging urgently in her locker. On the floor is her navy canvas backpack, practically every inch of which is covered by pins with this or that social justice slogan—COEXIST written in symbols from different religions, STRAIGHT BUT NOT NARROW within a pink triangle, and CHILDREN BY CHOICE with a smiley face, among others. I pick up the bag and let it dangle from my wrist. I'll never understand how Chloe just dumps her stuff on whatever grime-encrusted surface is nearby.

"Greetings," I say, announcing myself.

"Found it!" She pulls her head out of her locker and holds the box aloft triumphantly—store-brand hair dye in a color called "Blue Razz!" The model on the box looks like Violet Beauregarde from *Charlie and the Chocolate Factory*, after she's chewed the blueberry gum, while also performing a musical number from *Chicago*.

"Good?" she asks.

"Works for me."

"Where's the Protector of All Things Astrid and Killer of All Things Fun and/or Inappropriate?"

I roll my eyes. "Come on."

"Sorry, I meant your boyfriend." Truce or no truce, Chloe still takes the opportunity to give Mohit a little dig where she can.

"Jazz band."

She takes her bag from me and slings it over her shoulder. "Great, so your personal stylist can work in peace today."

"You *could* cut him some slack. Like occasionally. Just saying."

Chloe's already halfway down the hall, and I hustle to keep up with her, even though my right leg aches a little. She pauses by the stairwell while I catch up. "I'll cut him some slack when you're dead. In the meantime, we have living to do."

It never sounds harsh when Chloe says it. It just sounds honest.

We walk back to Chloe's place, which is empty except for Stanley, her crusty old beagle mix. "Hi, Stan," she says, nudging him with her foot as we enter the apartment. He whines at us. "He's not adjusting that well to the current living arrangement." Annalisa, one of Chloe's moms and the dog person in the family, moved out over the summer for a trial separation from Chloe's other mom, Cynthia. I can empathize with Stanley, since my father moved out when I was twelve.

Stanley trails us into the bathroom.

"Shirt off," Chloe orders me. "Sexy, huh?"

Chloe and I have been friends since middle school, when it became readily apparent that if there are two kids in your whole school who can't pick the latest boy band members out of a lineup and want to play word games and talk about science, they should probably team up.

In the bathroom, Chloe kicks aside various hair dryers and curling irons and mildewed washcloths and drops a towel on the floor by the tub so I can kneel on it.

"It's clean," she says. "I know with whom I am dealing."

I'm not actually *that* much of a germophobe. I mean, I am, sort of, but not clinically or anything. It started with an episode of *Shark Tank* Chloe and I watched several years ago, in which two start-up bros from MIT pitched a product that was essentially a disinfecting pod for cell phones, and they had all this data on how much fecal matter is lurking on your phone. Your crap is all over your phone, in other words. That kind of thing is hard to get out of a person's head. My head, anyway.

My head, which is spinning a bit now, like I've just stepped off a carousel that was moving a little too fast. I kneel on the towel and take some deep breaths. Chloe gently eases me under the faucet. She massages my scalp like she works in a hair salon. Then she towels me off, settles me on the edge of the toilet seat, and starts combing out my tangles.

As soon as the first snips of hair hit the floor, I feel lighter.

When most of my hair is on the floor around my feet, Chloe uses an electric shearer to get the back even. It's not a buzz cut like she gave me last time, when my hair started falling out in huge clumps, but it's on its way: a soft, boyish pixie, the front a little bit longer across my forehead. She admires her work.

"Good, right?"

I have to hand it to her—she's really very good at this. Years of YouTube self-haircut videos and experiments with varying degrees of success, coupled with tutorials from her "hairy godmother," Steve—Chloe's mothers don't believe in God-with-a-capital-G either, but they did assemble a cast of friends to teach her important life skills, such as cutting hair—and Clo has become quite reliable with a pair of scissors. She even does the thing where she holds up a chunk of hair and comes at it from an angle, although I have a feeling that might be more for show than for any actual effect.

"Hey, if the whole astrophysicist thing doesn't work out for you, you should really consider a career as an aesthetician," I say.

"And if this whole brain tumor thing doesn't kill you, you should really consider a career as a comedian."

"Fair."

Chloe turns my head gently to check each side. She nods, satisfied, then cracks open the box of dye and pulls on a pair of rubber gloves.

6.

OUR APARTMENT SMELLS LIKE FISH WHEN
I get home hours later. Delightful. I wrinkle my nose and follow the scent into the kitchen, where Mom is taking a dish of
salmon out of the oven.

"It smells in here."

"Keen observation, my girl." Mom turns around. "Whoa!
Look at you!"

"Chloe."

"I assumed." She kisses my forehead, then steps back and
examines my hair, fluffing it with one hand while she considers my new look. I duck out of the way. "Chloe learns how to
do this stuff online?"

I pull up a chair at the kitchen table. "And from her hairy
godmother, Steve. But yeah, she's sort of obsessed with You-
Tube how-to videos."

Mom stares at me, her brow furrowed. "You know what,
though?"

"Yes, Mother?"

"I like it. I really do. It suits you. You know I'm not massively into the artificial hair colors, but . . . what can I say? The blue works."

"Thanks." I nod toward the salmon. "The kitchen's going to stink for days, you know."

"Omega-3s!" She turns back to the fish and starts fussing over it. "The better for a healthy brain!"

"A little bit late for that, don't you think?"

Mom pauses. From behind, I watch her back tense and relax and tense again. Even without saying anything, I know she's focusing on her breath for a moment, her way of collecting herself. Then she turns to me.

"Astrid, I understand that you're cutting your hair off in anticipation of losing it again." Her voice is calm and flat. My mother is nothing if not a master of her own emotions, ninety-nine percent of the time. "I get that you are preparing yourself for what's next. But for my sake, and Liam's, and frankly your own, how about laying off the total morbidity just for a night, huh?"

I swallow. I want to object, since it's my life and my death and I should get to react however I want to react. But then I think about the sound of my mother's grief in the bedroom that night after our last visit to Dr. Klein, and the look on her face—absurdly full of hope—whenever she talks about the stupid clinical trial. It's hard for me to begrudge her what hope she has left. I'll be dead, after all. And she's going to be the one left behind.

The front door opens and Liam comes bounding into the

kitchen, smelling of soccer practice, all little-boy sweat and mud.

"Whoa, whoa, shoes off in the hall, mister!" Mom says.

Liam ignores her, just romps over to me and throws his arms around me. "Your hair is crazy!" he exclaims, ruffling it just like Mom did a minute ago. I mind it less coming from my little brother.

I breathe in his musty smell. "You stink, kid." He does, but I love it. "Want to bowl a round while we wait for dinner?" Liam's face lights up like he's just been told he's going to Disneyland, which makes my heart contract.

"Clean yourself first!" Mom says over her shoulder as we bound out of the kitchen. "And you only have ten minutes!"

I get the Wii set up in the living room while Liam scrubs down.

"All right," I say, handing him a controller when he reappears in pajama bottoms and a T-shirt. "Lightning-round bowling."

"That's not a thing."

"Whatever. I just meant, let's do this fast. Before dinner."

Liam bowls first, and he's much more expert at maneuvering the Wii controller than I am. His little Liam-like avatar bounces on the screen, and then he sends the ball straight down the center of the alley. Strike.

"Shit, dude," I say.

"Quarter in the swear jar!"

I roll my eyes. "Come on. That's only for when Mom catches us swearing, Lee."

Liam's blue eyes are wide and twinkly, and for a moment, it feels as if he's looking at me like he's never seen me before, like I'm not the sister he's never known his life without. There's a smudge of dirt on his forehead that tells me he didn't quite wash up the way Mom intended him to.

"Give me one free swear?" I whisper. "Our secret?"

He gives me an earnest thumbs-up. This kid, I'm telling you. I love the guy.

I bowl, first a two, then a goose egg. Liam giggles.

"Hey!" I say. "Don't laugh at the cancer patient! I should get a handicap or something. Brain tumor, automatic five-point bonus."

His smile dissipates, and I immediately regret mentioning the brain tumor.

"I was kidding, Lee. It's a joke."

He stares at the floor and mutters something.

"What? I can't hear you when you mutter like that." His teacher says he does it in class, too, more and more frequently, withdrawing into himself.

He raises his voice only slightly. "I said, do you only want to play with me because you got your tumor back?"

I put the controller down. "Bro, come on."

He won't make eye contact with me, so I pat the couch next to me and wait for him to saunter over on his own time. Eventually, he perches next to me, leaving plenty of air between our bodies. "I always liked playing with you. BT and AT. Before Tumor and After Tumor."

"Not true."

"It *is* true, Lee!" Realizing that arguing with an eight-year-old about this is not going to yield any satisfactory outcomes, I try a different approach, one Mom has always drilled into us—*feelings*. "Okay. I'm sorry. How does it make you feel when I don't play with you as much?"

He shrugs. "I miss you. And I feel like when you weren't sick, you didn't have time for me."

I resist the impulse to defend myself. It's not exactly accurate, but he's not totally wrong either. I think back to the last year, my good year, and all the time I spent away from home, exploring the city with Mohit, lying on the floor of his bedroom, talking nonsense, slipping back into the apartment after Liam was already asleep. Mom let me get away with it, probably because she'd almost lost me once for real, and losing me to a boyfriend didn't seem nearly as objectionable. When I wasn't with Mohit, I was with Chloe. So I can see Liam's point.

"I didn't mean to abandon you, kid. You know, when I finished my treatment the last time, it was kind of like having a new life. And I wanted to do all the living I could. Does that make sense?"

He shrugs. "I guess."

"But I didn't mean to leave you hanging. I always want to spend time with you. You're my favorite brother."

"I'm your *only* brother."

"Okay, well, that makes you lucky, because the competition for favorite is not that stiff."

He sticks his tongue out at me. "Your hair looks crazy."

Mom clears her throat, and I wonder how long she's been hovering at the living room entrance. Her eyes are glistening a little bit, which makes me think she's been there for a few minutes, just watching. "Dinner, guys."

In bed later, I think of Liam with his big eyes staring at me across the dinner table like a freakin' lost puppy. Goofy, sweet Liam. Hopeful Liam. Next year, or next month, or whenever the end comes, he'll be the kid with the dead sister. In school, other kids will watch him for signs that he's coming undone. He'll come home to a sad mom who will buy him too many Christmas presents to make up for how absent she's been. He'll become the worst kind of only child, the kind who's lonelier than if he'd never had a sibling in the first place, because he'll be living with the ghost of me.

I roll over and watch the neighbor's motion sensor light flash on. A raccoon going by, maybe, or a skunk, hunting in the trash cans for dinner.

I can't quiet my brain, thinking of my brother being *that* kid.

Dammit, Liam.

I guess it won't *kill* me to apply for the clinical trial.

7.

A FEW WEEKS AFTER MOHIT AND I MET IN homeroom, after we'd started accidentally-on-purpose finding each other at lunch and in the hallways at random intervals throughout the day, he told me he wanted to show me something I'd never seen before.

I raised an eyebrow. "You're pretty confident. How do you know I've never seen it?"

"I'm fairly certain."

I was intrigued, by him and his West Coast swagger and everything else. "So what's this something?"

"Just a thing. You'll have to wait and see." When he smiled, it was like death-by-dimples for me. (It still is.) Those deep pockets of joy dug into Mo's face, and I had to go along with whatever absurd plan he'd come up with.

That Friday evening, just as the sun was setting, he picked me up at my apartment and took me all the way downtown on the subway. It was a new thing, going on a "date," and my mother had looked apprehensive and enthusiastic and nostalgic, all at once, when she closed the door behind me.

"You're going to have to do better than this," I told him when we got off the train at a random stop on the Orange Line.

"Shush, shush. Just wait for it."

It was fall, still early enough that New England hadn't packed it in yet for winter and the streets were buzzing with couples taking an evening stroll along the cobblestones, wearing light, expensive-looking leather jackets and fashionably draped scarves.

I recognized the neighborhood, if mostly from movies directed by Ben Affleck. "I've *been* to the Bunker Hill Monument, if that's where we're going," I said as we huffed up Breed's Hill in the middle of Charlestown. "We went there in seventh grade. So if this is the thing I've supposedly never seen, you're wrong."

"Shhh. Don't ruin it."

"Fine, fine." I watched him from behind as we ascended through this quiet corner of Boston, lit softly by gas lamps. His hair was just a little too long in the back, ready for a trim. I already knew the contours of his face well enough that even from behind, I could picture where he had a fine spritz of pimples on his forehead, where one hair curled defiantly away from his eyebrow.

When we got to the top of the hill, the monument glistened in the fresh light of the moon, a huge sword rending the night sky in two. The wrought-iron gates around the park were locked.

"Oops," I said. "So much for that."

But Mohit shook his head. "You think I'd bring you all the way here at night only to show up at a locked gate?"

"Are we going to break the law?" I asked, as Mo led me around to the other side of the park.

He smiled at me. "Are you hoping the answer is yes, or no?" Then he stopped by a patch of shrubbery. "Here."

As Mo parted the shrubs, I saw that a section of the gate had been damaged, as though a car had careened into it years ago and no one had bothered to fix it. The damage left a gap barely wide enough for a small-to-average-size human to squeeze through. Mohit went first, then put a hand out to guide me through.

It was just the right amount of illegal—kind of bad, but not go-to-jail bad—to make me like him even more than I already did.

At the base of the monument, I caught my breath. My astrocytoma hadn't made itself known yet, but it was probably already growing there, blossoming inside my skull and wearing me down in ways I couldn't put my finger on. There were almost three hundred steps to the top of the monument.

"We're going all the way up?" I asked.

"I told you you hadn't seen this."

We put our cell phone flashlights on, lighting just enough to see two steps in front of us as we made our way up the obelisk. We climbed and climbed, not speaking. It was quiet enough that I could hear his breath a few steps ahead of me.

When we emerged at the top, he reached his hand out to help me up the last few steps, and it felt so normal—our hands in each other's. It sent the sparkliest shiver through me.

"There," he said, obviously proud. "See."

"Damn."

He took in the view and sighed happily. "If that doesn't make you believe in God . . ." he said, almost to himself.

I laughed, on impulse. I so rarely heard anyone talk about God and sound like they meant it. "I'm sorry. I didn't mean to laugh." I could feel my palms starting to sweat with nerves. Here I was, having a possibly romantic moment with a person I barely knew but very much wanted to know more, and I'd already managed to make a mockery of his apparent religious beliefs.

But Mohit just shrugged it off. "It's okay. I'm not offended."

"Okay, good." When the relief passed, curiosity—and a hint of boldness—replaced it. "Then can I ask you something? So you, like, believe in that? You look at that view and think it's all thanks to some higher omnipotent being?"

"Yeah, I do. That and architects. I'm guessing you don't?"

"I believe in the architects part."

He nodded as a small smile stretched across his face. "So there is a possible Venn diagram of our belief systems, then."

I pictured it: two overlapping circles. Faith in his circle;

in mine, I suppose, science. In the overlapping center, architects. Our Venn diagram.

"This view is my favorite thing about the East Coast so far," he said, going on. "Other than you, I mean."

Beneath us, the city unfolded in every direction. The brightly lit triangles of the Zakim Bridge stretched toward the sky, tucked between the skyscrapers. Tiny dots of headlights moved across the bridge, headed home and away.

On the other side, the rest of Charlestown was all low row houses and dim streetlights and blocks of public housing, and then the harbor.

We were standing just inches from each other, not touching, not speaking, but somehow it felt like our bodies were sending quiet bursts of energy back and forth.

"Good, right?" he said finally. "God, architects, whoever. Good?"

I couldn't help but smile. "Good."

8.

EVER SINCE THAT NIGHT, THE TOP OF THE
Bunker Hill Monument has been kind of our spot. So on Saturday, because it's unseasonably warm for October and you
never know how long fall is going to last, we make a pilgrimage.

I meet him at the entrance to the subway.

"Morning," he says, kissing me.

"Morning." I push my hood down, revealing my new hair,
and I watch as he takes it in. "So? What do you think?"

Cue uncomfortable pause.

"What?" I ask finally, even though I'm pretty sure I know
what he's going to say.

"Is that stuff permanent?"

I roll my eyes. "It's my hair. My life." My heart pounds a
little bit harder, the way it always does when I am aware that
I'm picking a fight, don't want to, and yet can't help myself.

"Why are you mad? All I asked was if it's permanent.
Is it?"

"I mean, that's your way of saying you don't like it. And

yes, it's permanent in the sense that it's not going to wash out in the shower, but it is impermanent in the sense that my hair is going to fall out again soon anyway. So then you won't have to look at it anymore."

"Okay, okay. No need to get melodramatic on me."

"Well, you could say something nice."

"So I have to say something nice now, even if I don't believe what I'm saying? Is that just a rule of having cancer—you earn the right to only ever have people agree with you and affirm your choices?"

I feel like I have emotional whiplash from how quickly this conversation has gone downhill. "You don't have to be a jerk about it."

Mohit hikes his backpack higher up on one shoulder. "I'm not being a jerk, I'm being honest. There's a difference."

"You're being a little bit of a jerk, though."

"And you're being a little bit childish. Is it a crime to have a preference for how my girlfriend wears her hair? I like your hair long, okay?"

"Wouldn't it be nice for you if I weren't about to go bald again, then."

He sighs deeply. "Can we go now, please?"

I give him a side-eye as we start walking into the subway. "Come on, Astrid," he continues. "You're beautiful, okay? Do I think you're more beautiful with hair that is not an absurd color that appears nowhere in nature? Yes. Sue me."

I chew my bottom lip. I want to be all, you know,

empowered and whatnot, and not care what my boyfriend thinks about my style choices. But I also want him to think everything I do is awesome. Most of all I want to stay mad, wallow in it for a little longer.

But when I turn to look at him, his curly black hair is sweeping across his forehead in a way that drives me crazy because whose hair does that with exactly zero effort and/or hair products? He half smiles at me hopefully, asking for permission for our fight to be finished. And just like that, I'm swallowed back in.

"I would sue you, but I can't afford a lawyer," I say, trying not to crack a smile myself.

"Your case doesn't hold any water."

"Okay, now I'm going to smack you."

"Then I'd really have the advantage in court."

I roll my eyes one more time, just to feel like I got the last word, and stalk off ahead of him down the escalator. Mo follows me, like I know he will, and we get on the inbound subway, heading toward our spot.

On the way up Breed's Hill, I have to pause to catch my breath.

"Stop here, Mo."

He's a few paces ahead of me on the path up to the base of the monument, but I'm completely spent from our walk. I bend toward the ground, hands propped on my knees.

"You okay?" He watches me with concern.

"I don't know if I can go to the top."

Mohit nods. He probably already knew that would be the case and was just humoring me so I wouldn't yell at him for underestimating what I could handle. He puts an arm around my shoulders and leads me over to a bench. I lean into his chest. The wind bites at my cheeks and reminds me of that very first night, when he brought me here and held my hand and I wanted everything to stay exactly the same forever. I didn't know then, although I should've guessed, that the only certain thing in this life is that nothing ever stays the same.

I slip my fingers through his. "Can I ask you something weird?"

"Please do."

"What does your dad say about reincarnation?"

He laughs. "I mean, are you under the impression that Indians just chitchat about reincarnation over breakfast?"

"That's not what I meant. Your dad sometimes counsels people in hospice, right?" Mo's father's religious duties mostly consist of officiating marriage ceremonies on the weekends, but I'm sure I've heard him mentioning also being occasionally on call to meet with Hindu patients who are at the end of their lives.

Now Mohit's face hardens as recognition sinks in. "Why are we talking about this?"

"Because I want to know. What does it mean, reincarnation? It's not *really* that you just get reborn in some other body. That's just what white people think it means, right? What do practicing Hindus believe?"

"You'd have to ask my dad, honestly. I don't really know."

"What do you think, though?"

He exhales, letting the breath vibrate through his lips. "Astrid, can we just enjoy a nice afternoon in the park without talking about mortality and the like?"

"'And the like,' really? What are you, an elderly British man now?"

"It sounded good in my head."

"Weirdo. Just tell me what you think."

Mohit settles back on the bench, his face locked in a pout. "I mean, it *is* about rebirth in another body. But it's like your present life and your present actions—they affect your next one. Hey, look." Some kind of large insect has alighted on his knee, a winged creature that looks practically medieval, with an armor of patterned gray on its back. It's probably just a fancy moth. Mo leans forward to inspect it, careful not to scare it away. "Whoa. Check out his exoskeleton."

"His what-now?"

"Exoskeleton. It's cool, right?"

"Mmm. Very," I say, mostly trying to appease him so he'll get back to reincarnation.

"Anyway." The creature flies off, and Mo watches it go. "What was I saying?"

"Your present life affects your next one?"

"Oh, right. Anyway, you don't know how much or how little you're going to suffer in the next life based on your current actions. Ideally, you're supposed to mature in each life, so eventually you can achieve freedom from rebirth.

Like, that's the ultimate reward. That you stop being reborn."

"And then you die-die?"

"I guess so. It's more like you just leave the cycle of birth and rebirth. Like you're not going to be reborn as a moth or something, but you're also not going to be reborn as a better human being. You're just, like, finished. But I don't really know, Astrid, I told you."

I chew on that, the idea of freedom from rebirth as a reward. I'd assumed reincarnation was a comforting concept— you get to try again at life, woo-hoo!—not a burden that you'd want to work toward absolving yourself of.

"You don't believe in any of that stuff, anyway," he says. "So why do you care?"

Mohit and I have argued the merits of faith versus science since we first met. He knows that in my family, we tend to scoff at the invocation of any kind of higher power as an explanation for anything. Science explains most things. And for the things it doesn't explain, I figure, it's only a matter of time before it will.

"I know," I say. "I'm just curious what you might be thinking. About what's going to happen to me, after." I stop there.

"After what?"

"You know what."

He shifts his body so he can look me in the eye. "I don't think about that. I think about how fast treatment options are changing. I think about the clinical trial you're going to be part of. And how we're going to shrink that tumor back to where it came from, just like the first time, and—"

"Mmmkay, whatever you say."

"Come on. Dr. Klein did it once already; there's no reason she can't do it again."

"Fine, I know. You're right." I huddle into him and take a breath. "But there's this thing I wanted to tell you about."

"Okay, so tell me. About the thing."

"It's called cryopreservation."

"Cryo-what?"

"Cryopreservation. It's . . . it's a new science, kind of. It's, like, freezing a body to preserve it at the moment of death."

Mo looks at me, his face contorted in complete incredulity. "I'm sorry, O science-minded, highly intelligent girlfriend of mine, but did you say *freezing a body*?"

"I know, I know. But it's a thing. When you die, they take your body and put it in some exceptionally cold freezer in a warehouse somewhere and preserve the tissue."

"For what purpose?"

"They don't really . . . know. Yet. But maybe . . ." I pause, thinking about how weird and unbelievable this is about to sound coming out of my mouth. "Maybe, one day, they could wake you up. I mean, not you, me. Could wake *me* up."

Mohit looks out across the park in front of us. A man in a neon vest is picking up trash on the other side of the lawn as though it's just another normal moment in another normal day. Which it is. A normal moment in a normal day. Except my astrocytoma is back, this time it's going to be the end of me, and I've just voiced out loud the crazy, fever-dream possibility that I could die without death being the last thing I do.

Neither Mo nor I say anything for a long time. I watch his face, the way his skin crinkles around the corners of his eyes, the way his Adam's apple pulses just a little in his throat when he swallows. I can see from the minute movements of his facial muscles that his brain is working inside his skull. This is what it means to be alive.

9.

LATER, ALONE IN MY ROOM, I OPEN THE CAMERA
on my phone and flip the lens so it faces me. Hello, Astrid. My
face looks gray and tired in the half-light, but the blue of
my hair is still bright. I shift to video mode and hit record.
I may as well start keeping track.

Things I'll miss when I'm dead (a partial list):
The view from the top of the Bunker Hill Monument
Lying next to Mo and talking
Lying next to Mo and not talking
Mo's Adam's apple
Wondering what will happen next

To be continued.

10.

TWO WEEKS LATER, I MAKE MOHIT DRIVE ME
to the extra appointment I made without my mother's knowledge.

"Why didn't you just talk to Dr. Klein about this at your
last appointment?" He meanders into the right lane without
signaling, inviting a loud honk from the driver behind him.
Driving isn't one of Mohit's core strengths.

I grip the door handle. "You are going to do your level
best to get us there alive, right? I'm already at risk for an un-
timely death as is."

"Yeah, yeah. I've heard it all before. Complain not to
your personal chauffeur."

"Fine." I check the right side mirror and over my shoulder
for impending collisions. We're clear. "And I didn't talk to
her about it last time because my mother was there, and I'm
not quite ready to introduce her to the concept of freezing
me, y'know?"

He shrugs. "Whatever."

I can tell he's still skeptical. Since I first brought up cryopreservation, Mohit has remained in heavy questioning mode, which is about right for him. What research has been conducted so far to indicate any chance of success with eventual reawakening? Would my whole body wake up and walk out of the lab one day, or would they map my brain signals to a computer? And, if so, does that mean the computer would behave like me? How much like me? What if the tissue is damaged in the process of preservation? If medicine doesn't advance enough to cure my brain tumor, then what's the point of waking up at all?

I have none of those answers. I'm not even sure the answers exist.

He pulls into the parking lot at the hospital. I lean on his arm on the way in the door. My pain's under control, now that Dr. Klein has managed to find the right meds to make me feel pleasantly numbed yet not totally loopy, but the weakness on my right side isn't getting any better, and I'm moving a little more gingerly than normal.

"You all right?" he asks as we go through the revolving doors. I ignore him and push myself to walk a little faster, a little stronger.

"So what gives me the pleasure of extra time with you today, Dr. Ayeroff?" Dr. Klein sits in the plush leather chair behind her neatly organized desk. We're in her office, not the exam room. We always sit in her office for "discussions."

"Well . . ." I glance at Mohit, seated in the chair next to me. Dr. Klein looks at him, too. He avoids both our eyes.

"I take it there's a reason your mother isn't here?" Dr. Klein squints at me. She knows me too well.

"I just want your opinion on something."

"My medical opinion or my wise-adult personal opinion?"

"Uh, both, maybe? I've been looking into . . ." I pause, suddenly aware of how ridiculous this is going to sound. But I'm here now. "I've been learning about cryonics?"

She shifts in the chair, nods. "Okay." She's not looking at me like I've lost a screw, at least.

"So I just wanted to know what you . . . know. About this."

"Well, Astrid," she says, "look." She cocks her head one way and then the other as though she's weighing her potential responses in her brain. "No one knows *that* much about cryonics. It's a very new field."

"But is it . . . I mean, could they, like, freeze me?"

Dr. Klein laughs a little bit. "'Freezing' isn't quite accurate, as I understand it. I think a specialist would tell you that it's a preservation process called vitrification, which is a little bit different from just shoving a body in a freezer. But yes, basically that's what we're talking about." She pauses, choosing her next words carefully. "Astrid, may I put on my doctor hat first here?"

I nod.

"I know you're discouraged by your latest scan. I am, too. But we're not at the end, not yet. We have some different options for chemo. And I really think you should consider this clinical trial."

Mohit nods enthusiastically next to me. "See, that's what I told her, too. It has real promise, right?"

"Mo, stop." I put a hand on his knee to calm him.

"It has promise," Dr. Klein concurs. "Is it a long shot? Any trial is, by definition. But is it as much of a long shot as cryopreservation? I wouldn't even put them in the same category. The former is reliant on the most advanced understanding we have of how cancers work, and the latter is . . ." She stops, considers it. "The latter is not."

"I might not even get a place in the trial, though," I say, "so I'm just considering my options. Do you think cryopreservation has—I don't know—any promise? At all?"

Dr. Klein stares at me for a long, quiet moment. Then she exhales. "Astrid, I'll tell you what I think. I think you're a scientist at heart. Cryopreservation is a far-out, long-game, future-future science. It's not going to save your life. You won't wake up a year from now in brand-new-with-tags condition."

"I know."

"I'm sure you do," she goes on. "This technology is so far beyond our current bounds of understanding that it seems more like magic than science. But I can't tell you it's impossible, because it isn't. It might not be *possible*, but it isn't *impossible*, not yet. That's what makes it science, not fantasy. I don't know if it's a good bet or not. No one knows. But I can understand why, as a scientist, you would be intrigued by it."

Mohit is silent in the car on the way home. I watch the city go by out the window: fall leaves drifting from their branches in a show of red and orange and yellow confetti celebrating the turn of another season; a couple pushing a baby in an SUV-sized stroller while a toddler bounds ahead of them on a scooter; two kids holding hands, our age-ish, the boy with a mop of red hair and the girl with long, beaded cornrows.

"How cold do you think it is right now at the Mount Everest base camp?" I ask Mo, apropos of nothing. "Like, at this time of year, is it winter already? Or same as here?"

"Huh? Why?"

"Well . . ." I've always wanted to see the Himalayas. I don't know why, really. I don't like hiking. Frankly, I don't even like the outdoors all that much. Mohit calls me "indoorsy," and it's not a lie. But I've always wanted to see those mountains, ever since I watched a documentary with my dad when I was little about all the people who've died on Everest. One of my favorite guidebooks to date is *The Trekker's Guide to Nepal*, which describes the trip to Everest in glorious detail.

When I'd first told Mohit about my fascination with big mountains I'll never climb, he'd promised to take me to the Himalayas one day. Most of his extended family still live in Gujarat, in the northwestern part of India, and some in Mumbai, but he has an aunt and uncle in Kufri, not far from the northern border, in a home built into the side of the Himalayan foothills. I imagine it's one of those places that takes planes and trains and automobiles and hiking by foot to get to. I've never been to a place like that.

"You've been there at this time of year, haven't you?" I press.

"Not really. I mean, the altitude at Mount Everest base camp is a lot higher than anywhere I've been. It's probably already winter there, yeah."

"So you can't really go there until spring, huh?"

"Astrid." Mohit understands now where I'm going with this. If I can't get there now, if we can't get on a plane tomorrow and go, I'll never see it.

I stare out the window again, imagining those icy hills cutting a path straight into the sky. "I'll miss it all."

Mohit shakes his head. "Come on. You can come to India with us next summer. Are you kidding? My parents would love that." It's true, Mr. and Mrs. Parikh have been inviting me on their annual family trip to India ever since Mo and I started dating, but that first summer I was in treatment, and last summer I had the internship with Dr. Klein. "Or the summer after. And all the summers—"

"Be real. There are no more summers."

"You don't know that."

My body aches. A dark shadow, bigger than any floater I've ever seen, crosses into my line of sight and blocks part of my peripheral vision on the right side. I close my eyes against it. This is what it will be like if I lose my sight, darkness on darkness. I mean, *when* I lose my sight, because that's what happens before you die from brain cancer. You lose all the things that help you interpret the world: sight, movement, appetite. Memory. Then breath.

Mohit is right, though. Maybe there are still summers ahead of me, just many years from now.

"What if I didn't have to miss it all? What if this death was just the next thing to happen, not the last thing?"

We stop at a red light. Mo turns to me and puts his hand on my leg. It still makes my heart race, Mohit's touch against my body. His forehead crinkles, deep in thought.

"What would you be, though? Would you still be a person?"

"What is a person?" I shrug. "Is a person more than our electrical signals, pinging back and forth?"

Mohit laughs. "Oh my gosh, Astrid." He always says "gosh," not "god." He only says "God" when he actually means it. "You are more than electrical signals. *That* I can tell you from personal experience."

"I don't know if I'd still be a person," I say. "Maybe I'd just be an Astrid-like avatar. Maybe I'd be Astrid's personality in another person's body. Maybe I'd be Astrid's electrical signals in an app. I have no idea. It's worth trying to find out, though, isn't it?"

He draws a long, deep breath, and my chest contracts.

"Yes," he says finally. "You are worth trying anything."

11.

WHEN CHLOE ANSWERS THE DOOR THE NEXT morning, she's already shoving Stanley back into the house so she can come outside with me.

"Come on, we're going out." She locks the door behind her.

"What's the rush, dude? I just got here."

"The moms are fighting about Christmas. Already. It's freakin' October. Whatever. I don't feel like listening to it."

Chloe had been predicting her mothers' split for a while before it happened——I mean, even I'd seen Cynthia and Annalisa arguing over the fact that Cynthia had put the near-empty milk carton back in the fridge, or that Annalisa had worked too late, or that Cynthia's mother was overbearing and intrusive, all of which seemed true. So it's not like it was a secret that they weren't getting along, but it still wasn't pretty when they actually separated.

"They're driving me bananas," Chloe says. "You'd think

they would just ask me how I want to divvy up the holidays this year, no? I'm not a child."

"Sorry."

Holidays with divorced parents suck, I get that. I mean, my father stopped doing any kind of "material celebrations" when he moved to a commune off the grid in Arizona, so those have been easy enough for me and Liam, but for a while after they split, my parents would fight over our school vacations. Mom couldn't afford to take us anywhere, but she would still want to do these elaborate *staycations*, where we'd play tourists and do all the touristy things you don't normally do (read: take a ridiculous Duck Tour through the city and hope you don't pass anyone you know from school along the route). And Dad would want us to come visit him in Arizona, saying Mom owed him the time because she had us all the rest of the year. They'd go around and around until they'd broker some kind of compromise—basically an annual trip to Dad's over the summer, when we could visit him and still have enough free time to come home and staycation before school started. It took a couple of years, but they finally figured out a routine.

But this is Chloe's first holiday season since the split, and her moms both have big families with what she refers to as "robust traditions," so I can already imagine it's going to get ugly.

"I mean, I'm old enough to have a say in things, aren't I?" She shoulders her bag. "Where are we going, by the way?"

"I don't know. I thought I was going to your house."

"Mom C's house, you mean." Chloe has always referred to her mothers as Mom A and Mom C, which started affectionately when she was little but later became a running joke—as in, "Where's Mom B?" Annalisa, Mom A, is staying with friends while she looks for a new apartment.

"It's still *your* house," I say.

But Chloe's not listening. She's already taking off down the block. "I just don't want to sit around and try to plug my ears anymore. The benefit of them splitting in the first place was that I didn't have to hear them bitching at each other all the damn time. Now they just do it over speaker phone, and I still have to listen to it." Then she stops in her tracks and looks at me. "Your hair looks truly excellent like that."

"It does, doesn't it?"

"Yeah. Who's your stylist?"

"Overpriced hipster salon. I should've gone to SuperCuts and saved my money."

"I'm LOLing on the inside, really."

"Not technically LOLing, then, is it?"

We walk in silence a few blocks, Chloe keeping several paces ahead of me but periodically pausing for me to catch up. Halfway up Mass. Ave., by the stationery store that always entices me to spend money on pricey notebooks I'll never fill and decorations for holiday parties I won't be hosting, Clo stops.

"Andy's?" she asks.

I'd already assumed that's where we were headed, since it's usually where we end up by force of inertia.

Andy's Diner looks like it's been unchanged since the 1970s, menu included, with cracking vinyl booths and revolving stools that list one way or the other. There's a small analog TV mounted in the corner, almost always playing some Boston sporting event or another depending on the season, and the waitresses are mildly unfriendly in an appealing way that makes you want to tip them extra so they'll feel better.

Our usual waitress, the one with long acrylic nails and teased bangs that have perhaps not been without hairspray since the mid-eighties, gives us a curt nod when we come in. We take the booth by the front window.

"You did your hair," the waitress comments dryly as she drops a pair of laminated menus in front of us. Her thick Boston accent—"*Yah did yah hayuh*"—was probably a prerequisite for getting a job here.

"*I* did her hair!" Chloe offers proudly. I can't help but let out a snicker at her not-so-humble humble-brag.

"For real?" The waitress looks impressed. "Don't waste that talent. You ladies want coffee, right?"

A few minutes later, we're both huddled over steaming mugs. I take mine black, have ever since freshman year. Chloe, meanwhile, douses hers in milk and sugar.

"Are you aiming for coffee, or molten coffee ice cream?"

"The latter, obvs."

I sip mine without replying for a moment, watching her attend to her glucose-filled concoction. "So getting back to your life," I say, "what do *you* want to do about Christmas? If they give you a choice?"

Chloe stirs her coffee and watches it spin toward the center, a liquid tornado. She shrugs. "I mean, whatever. They can duke it out over me. I don't care."

"It sounded like you cared twenty minutes ago."

"If they could be reasonable about the whole thing, then yeah. I'd probably go to New Jersey for Thanksgiving"— that's Cynthia's family—"and then be here for Christmas. My cousin will be in town from Milan, so obviously I'd like to see him."

"Does he still have the Italian-model girlfriend?"

She nods. "You know she's not actually a model, right? She's in med school. She's just very attractive. But yes, that girlfriend."

"Well, anyway," I say, "that seems reasonable."

The waitress comes back with our food: eggs over easy and bacon for me, a waffle with strawberries for Chloe. Plus more coffee for both of us.

"Right, except we did Christmas here last year. So Mom C is all like, 'It's my family's turn for Christmas.' Except they're Jews! So they don't even care!"

"I mean, they're the kind of Jews who have a Christmas tree."

"Right, but it's not exactly their holiday. You can't claim *everything*. I also went there for Rosh Hashanah. *Just* for dinner. They don't even go to synagogue."

"Sorry, Clo. It sucks."

"It must seem kind of lame to you. It sucks, but it's not, like, cancery."

"Glad I can provide you with perspective on your personal suckage. Suckiness is not a zero-sum game, though."

She takes a bite off a triangle of waffle soggy with syrup. "What exactly *is* a zero-sum game, anyway?"

"I don't really know," I confess. "It just sounded right."

"Not to change the subject or anything, but what did you decide about the clinical trial?"

My body fills with that weird adrenaline-rush feeling, like you're about to do something terrifying and want to step back from the edge of the cliff but know you can't. I don't know why I feel this way: talking to my best friend—about anything, really—shouldn't be terrifying. Chloe, of all people I know, won't judge me for my curiosity about cryopreservation. But I can't quite get over this feeling that every time I start to talk about freezing my remains, I sound like a total lunatic. Because who believes in this kind of shit?

I don't even believe in it. Except, maybe, possibly, I do.

"Dr. Klein sent my details in, all my test results. They have to decide if I meet the criteria. Even if I get a place in it, though . . ."

"What?"

"It's such a long shot, Clo. I could be getting the placebo, you know. And even if I'm not, these things almost never work well enough to actually help the people in the trial. It's more like helping doctors figure out how to help other people down the road."

"Right." She looks mildly dejected as she shoves the food around on her plate.

"Plus, it won't be pleasant. Dr. Klein said it could be even worse than chemo. Anyway, I don't know. I'm just thinking about, like, beyond that. My options."

Chloe narrows her eyes. "What does that mean?"

I launch into my explanation of cryopreservation, at least as much as I understand of it. Chloe listens with a strawberry perched on her fork, hovering midway between her plate and her mouth. She barely blinks until I'm done talking.

"So," I conclude, "basically, yeah. I'm thinking about preserving my dead body in a freezer in Arizona. Thoughts? Reactions? Questions from the crowd?" The adrenaline feeling escapes my body like air dissipating from a balloon while you try to tie it closed. I slice into an egg and watch the yolk seep out from the middle, a yellow puddle creeping toward the edge of my plate.

Chloe shakes the shock off her face and eats the strawberry. "I mean, I . . . It sounds . . ." She searches for a coherent thought.

I can't blame her for not knowing what to say. "Nuts?"

"No. I mean, yes. Kind of? But it also sounds . . . I don't know. Sort of awesome?"

It's exactly the reaction I expected from Chloe, and I could cry and hug her for it all at once.

"I guess the question is, How do they know if it'll work or not?"

"They don't," I say. "We don't."

Chloe chews her food for a long, thoughtful moment. "Shit, Astrid. I mean, you want to be a neuroscientist. If that's not going to happen . . ." She trails off.

"This is a way to be part of science, right?"

She sits back in the booth and stares at her plate for a minute. Finally, she nods. "Then you should go for it, this cryo-thing, or at least learn about it. What do you have to lose?"

"Right? If I'll be dead anyway, the worst that'll happen is . . . I'll stay dead."

Her face twitches a little at the word, but she brushes it off. "How much does the whole thing cost?"

Does health insurance cover body freezing? It suddenly occurs to me that in my curiosity about the possibilities of cryopreservation, I've never asked the most basic questions about how I'd pay for this.

Chloe's face melts condescendingly, which irritates me for a minute. "Astrid, you haven't found out how much it costs?"

"Not yet," I confess.

"Seems like kind of an important piece of information, no? I mean, not that you're not worth it, if it could actually work. But it could be, like, a lot of money."

"How much, do you think?"

"How would I know? Hold on—there's this thing called Google."

She starts tapping away at her phone. Almost immediately, I realize I don't want to know, because knowing will make it all the more real, and quite possibly make it totally impossible.

Across from me, Chloe squints at her screen, then lets out a quiet whistle.

"What?" I ask.

"Well, it's not cheap. Maybe they do a Black Friday deal."

"How not cheap are we talking?"

"Around thirty thousand."

"Thirty thousand U.S. dollars?"

"No, it's priced in Chinese renminbi." She makes a face. "Yes, U.S. dollars."

I laugh, only because it's so ridiculous. I could never get my hands on that kind of money. My mother certainly doesn't have it. It's just as well, really. I shouldn't get my heart set on some far-off, near-impossible possibility anyway.

Chloe taps her fingernails on the linoleum tabletop. "I mean, we *could* raise the money. If you wanted to."

"Funny. What are we going to do, organize a car wash for freezing my remains? A school bake sale to preserve my dead body?"

She waves me off. "Crowdfunding. On the internet, obviously. You'd just need, like, a vlog."

"A *vlog*?"

"A video blog. Hello? We make some videos about you and your story. We post them to a crowdfunding site."

"So basically Kickstarter for sick people?"

"Basically. We share your story. Other people share it. People send money. We get you a cryopreservation installment plan, if you will."

"That sounds insane."

"More insane than the idea of freezing your dead body to begin with? Because you're the one who brought this up."

I consider Chloe across the table, the sprinkle of freckles on the bridge of her nose that I was always jealous of when we were younger, and her hazel eyes that are green today to match her sweater, and her curly hair. She's my best friend, and she'd do anything for me. Including, apparently, using the internet to buy me a next-to-impossible possible future.

"What are you thinking about?" she asks.

"Just thinking."

Chloe nods. "Well, I'd give you the money if I had it. But since I don't . . . I give you the internet."

12.

THE SECOND TIME MOHIT AND I HUNG OUT
outside school, back in the fall of ninth grade, it was the night
of a Perseid meteor shower. He met me in front of my building
after jazz band rehearsal, just as the sun was setting, and we
returned to Bunker Hill Monument, because it already felt
like our spot, and because we knew it would have a good view
of the sky.

The park was lit only by a few flickering streetlamps.
We sat on a bench in the dark and angled our chins toward
the sky.

"Orion's belt," he said, pointing to the line of three stars
over our heads.

I followed the stars in their familiar path with my finger.
"And Draco's head."

"Nice one."

"My mother used to make me keep a sky journal," I said.
"Hence I can identify an uncanny number of constellations."

"Is a 'sky journal' a thing I'm supposed to know about?"

I laughed. "Not if you don't have hippie parents, I guess. You know, it was like, every night when she wasn't at work, we'd go outside to the exact same spot—it was the top of a hill near our house when we lived in the country—and I'd draw a picture of the sky in my notebook, where the moon was that night, what shape, and then we'd talk about our observations of how it was different from the night before. And she'd point out whatever constellations we could see."

He nodded, but I could tell he already thought I was weird. I guess his parents never made him keep a sky journal. He probably just remembered the constellations from when everyone learned about them in middle school. I liked thinking of Mohit in middle school, on the other side of the country, walking on the beach with friends, maybe going to music camp in the summers, living his very different life so far from mine before the moment when our worlds overlapped.

After that, he didn't say anything for a long while, longer than seemed possible or normal, but he was apparently not bothered by the silence, so I tried not to be, either. The wind picked up, and we inched closer to each other. I noticed; I assumed he did, too.

"Where's your dad?" he asked, when he finally spoke again. I didn't think I'd mentioned my father to Mohit; in fact, I was sure I hadn't.

"Why do you ask?"

"You talk about your mom all the time. She's a midwife, she makes you keep a sky journal—"

"Not anymore."

"Fine, not anymore. Sorry, is that an intrusive question? About your dad?"

"I mean, kind of?"

"Sorry," he said. "I have a habit of asking questions that other people seem to deem inappropriate. That's what my mother says, anyway. You don't have to answer."

"It's okay." It genuinely was. I liked that Mohit would ask the things other people wouldn't, and that he seemed to really want to know. "My parents split when I was twelve. Dad made some different lifestyle choices, I guess you could say. He wanted to live totally off the grid. My mom could do the hippie thing if it meant growing her own vegetables, but not, like, eschewing wifi."

"Eschewing wifi, huh? That does sound radical."

"Right? He moved to a commune in Arizona, and we moved to the city so my mom could be closer to work."

The truth is, my father left us because he fell in love. Not with another woman, in the predictable midlife-crisis kind of way, or with a man, which would've been at least understandable had it been the case. My father fell in love with the promise of a life free of attachments to the material world, from reliance on consumerism, from the "sickness that comes along with being tied to capitalism, and government, and mass-produced energy." Or something like that. He fell in love with a group of people who were collectively committed to living off the grid on a place called simply the Ranch, following the guidance of a frumpy white guy named Roger and showering infrequently. As far as I can tell.

To reach him now, we call a number that goes to the main lodge, which houses the only generator on the compound, and they get a message to him and he calls us back. Dad lives in a tiny house on the property with his new wife, Suzanne, and they don't have a phone of their own. Or internet. Or running water. But they have Peace and Love and Health, apparently. Or something along those lines.

It's not really as bad as I'm making it sound. Mostly it's just bizarre. But people make their choices, as my mother always says.

Mohit's eyes flicked over my face, considering me. Then he brushed his finger against my leg, so lightly it could almost have been an accident except I knew it wasn't, and I felt that same shiver that I'd felt the last time we were here together, when he'd reached for my hand at the top of the monument.

"Sucks that he lives so far."

I shrugged. "I mean, my brother and I visit him once a year or so. His place is pretty wacko, but it's not terrible. It's like camp. It's fine."

"Yeah. I know what you mean."

I got the feeling that he actually did know what I meant, even though I was fairly certain his parents were still married and his house had electricity. We went quiet again. I averted my eyes from his—it was too much to keep looking at him—and then, suddenly, the silence was too much, too. I pointed to his sax case. "How long have you been playing?"

"Since I was seven. I was barely big enough to hold it."

"Play me something?"

The request took him by surprise. "Here?"

"Yeah, here. You're the guy with the saxophone in the park. Why not?"

He opened the case and took the instrument out, cradling the pieces deftly the way I've seen my mother handle a brand-new baby. He put the mouthpiece in place, licked the reed. I liked watching him feel his way around the sax, the lightly tarnished brass looking well loved. I bet he could do it all with his eyes closed.

He started playing, a slow, beautiful, sad melody I didn't recognize.

He was good at playing sad songs.

Then a bright streak shot across the sky, and another, and another. The Perseids, pieces of burning comet debris, lighting up the night.

13.

ON SUNDAY, I WAKE TO MY PHONE VIBRATING
against the bedside table, which means I've either slept
through the scheduled "Do not disturb" function, which goes
until 9:00 A.M. on weekends, or someone (there are only two
possibilities, really) has called me multiple times in a row,
thereby disabling DND.

It's the former: 10:05, and Mo is calling.

"Mmm-hmmm," I mumble into the phone.

"Rise and shine, my beauteous princess!"

"Gross."

"Please, you love it."

I rub my eyes and open them wide against the light to
force myself awake. "What's up?"

"It might be the last beautiful day of the season. I think
we should go on an adventure."

It's the end of October. Any day now it could turn cold
and not turn back until practically May, and by the time the
warmth returns . . . who knows. Plus, I start chemo next

week, every Thursday afternoon for at least the next twelve weeks, which means my weekends will probably become a blur of lazing around with an emesis basin within reach. I assume Mohit is thinking of all this, even though he doesn't say so. He was around the last time; he remembers.

I look out the window. He's right about the weather. The cloudless sky is an unbelievably crisp blue against the reds and yellows of the leaves.

"But I'm tired," I whine. "How about you come over and we watch a movie in my bed?"

"I don't want to lie around inside, and neither do you!" Mo says.

"You're sure about that?"

"Quite sure. Listen, I have two words for you."

"So far it sounds like a lot more than two." I stretch out from under the covers with considerable effort.

"Two words, Astrid: Yankee. Cannonball."

"And that would be?"

"It's the last weekend of the season at Canobie Lake Park. Come on. How long has it been since you rode a roller coaster?"

"*Canobie Lake Park*? I haven't thought about that place since I was, like, twelve. We went there in middle school once."

"Exactly. You did, but I, alas, have never been, because as you know I spent my childhood on the superior coast, where we had, you know, actual Disneyland. We can get fall discount tickets today. I already looked online. Let us go relive the thrills of your youth with legions of middle schoolers."

"The thrills of my youth, huh? You're really in a poetic kind of mood today."

"I'm just thinking about kissing you at the top of the Giant Sky Wheel. It's so vintage."

Canobie Lake Park is forty minutes up 93 from Boston, just over the border in New Hampshire. Even that bit farther north, most of the leaves have already fallen. Bare trees stretch their branches toward the road.

Mo is driving, which I'll acknowledge he's getting better at, the more I make him chauffeur me around. We're in my mother's Honda, which she allowed us to borrow after only a moderate amount of cajoling. I got the sense that her desire to allow me any small pleasures that won't kill me outright overruled her desire to protect me every minute of every day.

I sit in the passenger seat with my feet up on the dashboard. Behind the wheel, Mohit has a small, peaceful smile on his face like he's thinking of something that's involuntarily making him happy. Every time I glance over at him, he seems to sense it, and shifts his eyes over to meet mine.

"Eyes on the road, partner," I remind him. Surprising for such a nice fall weekend, 93 is mostly empty, but still, I'd rather Mo not be so disarmed by my captivating beauty that he drives us off the road. I shift in the seat so my body is arched toward the driver's seat, closer to him. "Can I ask you something?"

"You just did."

"You're hilarious. If music doesn't work out for you, you should really consider stand-up."

"I don't know, the field for South Asian comedians is really competitive right now."

"You could hold your own with Aziz Ansari."

"Not with Mindy Kaling, though."

"True. Not with Mindy Kaling. Sorry," I say. "Anyway, I meant an actual question. You don't have to answer."

"Ask away, my beauteous princess."

"You can stop with the beauteous princess BS, you know."

"Fine, fine, ugly grouchy lady-in-waiting. What's the question, then?"

"Are you offended by the idea of cryopreservation?"

He doesn't answer for a long time, which is one of my greatest Mohit pet peeves. It's not that he's not listening, I've learned; it's just that he likes to think before he speaks. But the silence makes me nervous.

Finally, I can't take it anymore. "Hello?"

"I'm thinking. You know I'm thinking."

"I know, but . . . fine."

He clears his throat, turns the radio down. "Why would you think I would be offended?"

"Well, because of what you said about how the ultimate goal in Hinduism is to free yourself from rebirth. And with cryopreservation, I would be kind of opting *for* rebirth, in a sense. And maybe interfering with the natural process of things. So I was just thinking about how you might, I don't

know, feel weird about that. Or your parents would, or . . .
Hindus in general."

"I can't really speak for Hindus in general."

"I'm aware of that."

He goes on thinking for another long moment. "Well,
you're not just asking about Hinduism, right? Hinduism has
one set of beliefs about mortality and the afterlife, but really,
every faith has its own corresponding set, and they all tend to
involve theories of what happens to the soul after death. So
you might ask the same question of a person of any faith. It's
not a Hindu-specific concern."

"Fine, I get that. But you and your family are basically the
only religious people I know, so I'm asking you."

Mo laughs. "Got it. So now I speak not just for all Hindus
but also for all people of any kind of religious faith. No pressure."

"Come on. I'm just curious if *you*, Mohit Ramchandra
Parikh, are personally offended by the idea of science manip-
ulating life after death. And don't sit there quietly for another
ten minutes, please."

He shakes his head and chuckles to himself, like his girlfriend and her existential questions are just *that* amusing.

"Okay, here's what I think. Personally, I believe in re-
specting other people's beliefs. Your atheism doesn't offend
me. But, I mean, if it were me, I think I would worry about
what would happen to my consciousness. I would question if I
was impeding the process of rebirth if I were, sort of, *trapped*,
in a sense. Trapped in this in-between state, dead but not dead.

That, and I think it's very unlikely to work. So I'd worry that you were in this in-between state for no good reason, because nothing would ever come of it."

"But what if it gave you a chance to see me again? Even much later?"

Mohit turns to me, eyes now fully off the road. "Astrid, I would do anything to see you again—you know that. I just believe in a plan."

"God's plan?"

He smiles, looking back to the road. "I know you think it's ridiculous, but yes."

"I just don't get it. You really think there's something controlling all our moves here? Mapping it all out? Not just in this life but, like, after our deaths?"

"You know what I believe. We have agency, we make choices, but yes, there is a bigger plan."

"But what if . . . I don't know. What if the plan is wrong?"

"That's the point of faith, Astrid. You have to figure it's not wrong."

The Yankee Cannonball is one of those old wooden roller coasters that creaks while you work your way up the hills. We ride it three times in a row. Mohit grabs his phone out of his pocket and insists on taking a video of us screaming the whole way around, even though there are multiple huge signs that say, THE TAKING OF PHOTOGRAPHY OR VIDEO ON THE

YANKEE CANNONBALL IS STRICTLY PROHIBITED. Like when he snuck us into the Bunker Hill Monument on our very first date, it's exhilarating to break the rules just a little bit, even though I'm afraid he'll get us kicked off the ride, or at the very least drop his phone and lose it forever in the grassy restricted zone below the coaster. He manages to avoid both.

The first time through, I grip the safety bar with every ounce of strength my hands can muster and squeeze my eyes shut against the twists and drops. But the second time, I watch each hill approach, take in the feeling of losing control as we creak toward the top, and then let go of the bar—tentatively at first, then completely. The air whooshes past my fingertips as Mo snaps a selfie of us with our arms aloft.

After the third time around, though, my skull is starting to vibrate and I feel like my brain stem could use a rest. We sit for a few minutes and share a Coke on a bench by the bumper cars. Mo plays back the video. The footage is wobbly and ridiculous, our faces going from anticipation to fear to involuntary exhilaration and back again with every dip and curl of the ride.

I lean back on the bench and close my eyes against the bright day.

"What's next?" he asks.

In truth, my head is pounding, and my vision is getting twinkly. I don't want to ruin his adventure day with my stupid brain cancer, though. "Skee-Ball?"

"Excellent."

The wooden Skee-Balls knock against the ramp with a satisfying *thwack*. I used to be very good at this game, my skills honed over years of county fairs when we lived in the country and their parking-lot equivalents once we moved to the city. We're kitsch people, Mom and I—we've never driven by a carnival we didn't pull over for. But today I can't quite focus, can't get my arm to aim exactly in the right direction or with the right amount of force. I throw a bunch of lousy tens in a row, then one twenty.

"Nice!" Mo says.

"Sure, thanks," I mutter.

He fills the silver coin slots with another dollar's worth of quarters, and the balls roll out the chute. "Go for it. One more round, champ."

My right arm throbs along with my head now, and my vision is all Christmas lights and blurred edges like I'm viewing the world through an Instagram filter. Still, Mohit looks so hopeful. I wrap my fingers around one of the balls and lob it up the ramp.

It's too much. The ball bounces off the wall of the Skee-Ball machine and back down the ramp toward us with a fair amount of force.

"Whoa, careful." Mo tugs me out of the way just before I take a wooden ball to the skull, and the jarring movement causes me to drop to one knee.

"Sorry. Sorry," I say.

Mohit kneels next to me. "Hey, you okay?"

I pull myself up and perch on the edge of the ramp, rubbing my temples. "Yeah. I'm fine. I just got . . . off-kilter."

"Want some water?" He unscrews his bottle and offers it to me.

I take a few breaths and swallow some water while I wait for things to stop spinning quite so much. Mohit is quiet, watching me, waiting for a sign.

After a moment, I force a smile in his direction. "I just didn't want you to beat me quite so badly."

"Figured as much," he says. "You all right?"

I nod.

His face brightens. "Cool. So what next? Overinflated basketballs? I know you never met a rigged arcade game you didn't love."

I hesitate, and Mo seems to sense it.

"It's okay," he says. "I mean, if you want to go."

My throat is so dry. I take another sip of his water, but it seems like it absorbs immediately without any moistening effect. Everything aches.

"Can we? I think I'm just overexerted. Or I broke my brain on the Cannonball."

Mohit slings his backpack over one shoulder. "Of course. It's fine. Let's go. Don't want you to be overexerted." Then he starts off, leaving me resting there on the Skee-Ball ramp.

I stand up gingerly, assess my balance—the world has mostly righted itself—and follow after him, but he's practically out of sight. When I finally catch up, he's hanging out by the arcade exit.

"Uh, thanks for waiting."

He looks at me kind of dully. "Of course." Then he heads off again, toward the parking lot, with me trailing behind him.

"What was that?" I ask when we're both settled in the car. As we drive through the parking lot, Mohit turns the radio on, a Top 40 station. He hates Top 40.

"What was what?"

"That. You stalking off, leaving me behind. What's the matter?" I turn the volume down.

"I was listening to that," he says, turning it back up again.

"Parikh, come on. You hate this crap. Why are you acting like a weirdo?"

"I'm not. I'm just—"

"I mean, objectively, you are."

"I planned the day, Astrid. For you."

His words settle in the air around me. I feel something seething in the pit of my stomach, anxiety, anger, a mix of both, and I swallow, trying to calm it. On the radio, some pop star is whining about how some guy never called her back. I flick it off.

"You mean you planned the day for *you*."

He grips the wheel. Fighting with Mo while he's driving, given his vehicular deficiencies to begin with, is probably unwise. But he started it.

"What are you talking about? I'm not the one who cares about roller coasters and arcade games. I was trying to do something nice for my girlfriend. And you couldn't even muster the energy to—"

"To what, exactly? To help you fulfill your dreams of being World's Number One Boyfriend? Sorry my terminal diagnosis got in the way, Mohit."

He laughs. "Yup, there it is."

"There's what?"

"The cancer card. I was waiting for it."

"The *cancer card*? Are you freaking kidding me?"

"You seemed fine this morning. You were fine on the roller coaster three times in a row. Then suddenly you're like, 'We have to go home right this minute. I can't possibly stand up for another moment.' Come on. You're just so . . ." He trails off, shaking his head as he glances over his left shoulder to pull us onto the interstate.

"Yes? Please, by all means, tell me what I am so much of."

"I get it, okay? I get that you have cancer, believe me. I was there the last time, as you may recall. But does everything have to be so . . . melodramatic?"

I let that sit with us. The haziness in my head, the blurring in my vision, the aching radiating from my skull and pulsing up and down my spine—but sure, that's melodrama. I want to open the car door and get out, right now. I don't. Instead I stew.

"Astrid," he says when the silence has apparently become too much for even him to bear.

"What."

"I didn't mean that."

"Yes you did. You did mean it. I'm sorry I'm such a burden on you, believe me, Mohit."

"You're not a burden. I just—"

"No, Mo, I am. I am a burden. And I am going to continue to be a burden." He starts to try to interrupt, but I put my hand up, shake my head, and he stops. I go on. "The thing is, I can't really do anything about being a burden. I can't, like, magic myself back to normal. So you make a choice, okay? Because I have enough to deal with, and I can't also deal with having to pretend I feel awesome all the time for the sake of protecting my boyfriend's feelings. Anyway, I thought we were past all that. So make a choice."

He waits to respond, maybe giving it a minute to see if I'm really done. I am. I am really, really done.

"What choice," he says finally, almost under his breath.

I don't respond.

"Astrid, what choice?"

"You know what choice, Mo."

"I just thought we could, you know, do something fun. And normal. Like regular teenage people."

"I know you did, but I'm not a regular teenage person. I am, and I'm not. There's nothing I can do about it."

We drive most of the rest of the way in quiet.

14.

SOMETIMES IN THE SCHOOL CAFETERIA, I HAVE
this sort of out-of-body experience like I'm watching a
movie of my teenage life, in which someone who looks just
like me plays the protagonist and my classmates fill the roles
Hollywood and history have made for them: the jocks wearing
their varsity jackets, the theater geeks quoting the latest
Broadway hit, the bilingual kids telling secrets in languages
I don't speak, all around their preordained tables, over limp
iceberg lettuce and oven-baked french fries.

On Monday, in the movie of our lives, Chloe slides onto
the seat across from me and looks me up and down. "You
look kind of like shit."

"Thanks."

"Just keeping it real, friend. You okay?"

I feel considerably better than I did yesterday afternoon,
physically, anyway, but I don't respond.

"Hello." Chloe is frowning at me, holding a flaccid fry
near her mouth. Ketchup drips off onto her tray. I can't tell

Chloe about arguments with Mohit, ever. Their relationship is too delicate as is for me to give her any ammunition to use against him later, when things are good between us again.

"I'm fine." I shovel a mouthful of sloppy joe into my face and glance toward the door one more time. Mo has this lunch period today. I don't know why he hasn't shown up yet. I sent him a text a few minutes ago—*Are you dining today?*—but I haven't heard back.

"So I told the moms I was boycotting all holidays, like indefinitely, if they continued to act like children," Chloe says.

"And?"

"They basically relented. I mean, they said I could have a say in the matter but that there had to be some *equity*." She puts air quotes around the word "equity," like the whole concept is a farce. "Are you listening to me?"

I guess I look distracted. I can't help it. "Sorry." I look up from my phone, which I keep checking for signs of Mohit, even though there are none. "I am listening."

"I realize my problems are boring compared to yours."

"I'm sorry, Clo. Seriously. That's great, then. You can go wherever you want for Christmas."

She shrugs. "Yeah. And have one of my mothers inevitably be irritated with me. I guess I have to accept a certain amount of irritation now, right?"

"Or they have to accept that they put you in this position and just deal with it."

"Or that." She hunts around in her bag for something. "So I got you a present." She unearths a book from the depths of the bag and passes it across the table to me. It's a used travel guide, but not for a specific country or city. This one has a stretch of U.S. interstate on the cover. It's called *The Top 50 Roadside Attractions in the United States*. I flip through the listings of all the best kitsch within striking distance of American highways.

"Cool, right?" Chloe says. "I found it on the curb yesterday."

I put it down momentarily and wipe my hands with a paper napkin.

"Oh, Astrid. I already doused it in hand sanitizer."

"Phew. Thank you." I open to a random page. "The world's largest Pez dispenser is in Burlingame, California. Did you know that?"

"Now I do."

"Seven feet, ten inches tall, in the shape of a snowman." I skip around to a few more chapters, pausing to read briefly about some supernatural crop circle or giant ball of twine. "Thanks, Clo. This is kind of cool."

"Well, so, I had a thought."

"Just the one?"

"What if you could actually see some of these places you're so obsessed with reading about? Like, what if we could make it happen?"

"Right. Between the chemo sessions and the hospitalizations for the clinical trial, my winter and spring are looking pretty open. Let's just book a couple international flights."

"I'm serious, Astrid. We don't have to go to the Himalayas. The Pez dispenser, for example, is on our present landmass.

Or . . ." She takes the book out of my hands. "Lucy the Elephant, in Margate, New Jersey. Even closer. We can stop there on our way to Arizona."

"Arizona?"

"Sedona, to be precise. Isn't that where your cryopreservation facility is located? Hear me out. What if we use the vlog idea, as a start, to get you to there? Just for a visit, so you can make an informed choice. You wouldn't have to commit. You wouldn't even have to raise that much money yet—just enough to get us to and from Arizona."

"Us?" I raise an eyebrow at her.

"Think I'm letting you go alone? Consider it a once-in-a-lifetime road trip."

"Literally."

"Literally."

The idea of something to do—a trip to plan, an adventure to embark on that has nothing to do with being sick—does sound enticing. And I *do* like the idea of seeing where I might end up if I go the frozen-body route. But the vlog part makes me squirmy.

"I just don't know about this whole crowdfunding thing. Putting my personal life on the internet? Like, on video?"

"You get to pick your boundaries, though. You craft the narrative. That's what all the internet personalities do. You give people just enough to make them feel like they know you. That's why they pay attention. And if they're paying attention, they're donating. Trust me."

I let out a sigh.

"Is that a yes?" she asks, her eyes fixed on me.

I don't get to answer, though, because my phone starts vibrating against the table. I grab it, assuming it's Mo, but it isn't. It's my mother. Which is weird, because she never calls me at school. She actually believes we don't even look at our phones at all during school hours. Or I thought she did, anyway, but there she is, calling.

"Uh, hello, Mother. Everything okay?"

"Astrid?"

"Yes, this is she. Clearly."

"Dr. Klein just called." Mom sounds frantic. "They'll take you in the trial."

I pick the restaurant—Greek—because Mom insists on going out and I don't want to kill her buzz. We're already dipping triangles of pita in creamy tzatziki when Mohit finally shows up. I texted him again after Mom delivered the news, but I didn't actually expect him to show up to dinner; he's been MIA since our fight yesterday. He seems flustered when he arrives, his sax case in one hand and sheet music in the other in a haphazard pile, instead of neatly tucked into a manila folder like usual.

"Hi." He gives me a quick kiss. "So! Great news!"

"Isn't it? What are you having?" Mom passes a menu across the table to Mo, who takes the seat Chloe left open next to me. "It's time to celebrate."

I tell myself, for the umpteenth time since we left home

an hour ago, that this "celebration" is for my mother, because she needs every little victory. I force a smile around the table, playing the dutiful, grateful daughter/patient.

Mohit orders the eggplant wrap and a Coke. "Where've you been?" I ask him quietly when he hands the menu back to the waitress.

"Nowhere. Just had some stuff to take care of." Then he gives me a stern look that reads, *Please don't get into this now.* Turning back to the rest of the table, he raises his voice to cover any awkwardness. "Hey, this is great! You're in the trial."

Mom insists on making a toast to my "future health." Several neighboring diners glance curiously in our direction, hoping to catch a glimpse of the sick person, I guess. I shrink a little bit into my seat and try to tamp down my embarrassment.

I know Mom's excited. I know she's hopeful. But it all feels like a joke. This recognition crystallized in my head the moment Mom announced the "good news" and I realized my heart was sinking instead of soaring. The trial is just one more step on the long march toward my premature demise. It's days or weeks in the hospital, hours and hours of treatments and tests, of being poked and observed and watching Mom wait anxiously for results. And it won't work. They never do. I wish I didn't even have the option.

After dinner, Mom drives Chloe and Mohit home. I let Liam sit in the front so I can squeeze next to Mohit in the middle seat and slip my fingers between his. He reciprocates but doesn't look at me, just stares out the window while I search the back of his head for clues. The dark hair curling against the collar of his jacket gives nothing away.

When we pull up in front of the Parikhs' house, I walk to the front door with Mo. He pulls his keys out and then turns to me. "Look, I'm sorry about yesterday. I was kind of a jerk, huh?"

"Little bit?"

"Yeah. About your question, though. You *know* my choice, right?"

I don't say anything. I'm not going to do the work for him.

"Astrid, I choose you. I'll always choose you. In sickness and in health."

"We're not married, Mo. You don't have to say that." Still, my heart feels like it's expanding with the words.

"I know I don't have to. But I want to. I choose you. Okay?"

Mom beeps. I'd forgotten she was waiting for me. I kiss him on the cheek and say good night.

15.

CHEMO. HELLO AGAIN, OLD FRIEND.

Dr. Klein promises it won't be as bad as the first time, partly because the drugs have improved even in the last year and a half, and partly because my body will adjust more quickly the second time around. As with anything else, you get better at it with time. I'm so glad to be improving at ingesting toxic chemicals in an attempt to stop my body from attacking itself.

So on Thursday afternoon, after school, I settle back into one of the familiar blue loungers in the familiar stale chemo lounge. Mohit would've come with me, but he had another mysterious "thing" to take care of, and Mom couldn't change her shift, so I'm here alone, much to my mother's distress. I told her it was fine. To be honest, it's more than fine. I don't really need anyone else to bear witness to my official return to Cancer Patientdom.

Today's nurse, Colette, hooks my line in and gives me an

encouraging pat on the arm. She's new here. Or, at least, new since I was here last.

"You want a magazine, sweetness?"

"No thanks." I have actual homework in my bag, but I probably won't bother with it.

"All righty. Let me know if you need anything."

I respond to a text from Mom, checking in, then pull *The Trekker's Guide to Nepal* out of my bag. It's become comfort reading at this point, like *Harry Potter* used to be when I was a kid. I flip through the well-worn pages, rereading the section about flying into Lukla, the closest airport to Everest, widely regarded as the scariest landing strip on the planet.

I lose myself in the Khumbu region for a while, and when my eyes are starting to strain from reading the cramped print, I browse the channels on the flat-screen mounted to the opposite wall. On the Discovery Channel, there's a program about free soloing—rock climbers who scale insane-looking rock walls with no ropes or harnesses whatsoever. In other words, they're one tiny mistake from plummeting to their deaths. Perfect. I really don't know what it is about the idea of climbing sheer rock faces or huge Himalayan ice-encrusted peaks that is so fascinating to me, dedicated indoorswoman that I am, but they get me every time.

I sit back and follow the exploits of a young guy named Aidan Wallace—mid-twenties; unshaven with big, goofy ears; no attachments in his life except a van he lives in and a girlfriend who's a climber, too—as he free solos some of the toughest rock walls in North America. He looks earnestly at the camera, a stunning southwestern landscape of red rock and desert sunset behind him.

"Sometimes, when you're up there alone, with no ropes, it feels like you're just stepping into the void."

Cut to him inching up Half Dome at Yosemite, nothing but a centimeter or two of bare fingertips between him and the empty, open air. As I watch, I momentarily forget where I am, who I am, the toxins pumping into my blood. I inhale a breath and hold it there; my heart pauses; the room seems to pitch sideways. Then he's up, over the lip of the cliff, onto the summit, his arms lifted toward the bright sky in triumph. Still alive.

"Boo!" Chloe bounces into the room, and I jump about a mile out of my recliner. "Sorry, didn't mean to scare you."

"What are you doing here, Clo?"

She sits down in the empty recliner next to me. "Keeping you company."

"Did my mother call you?"

Chloe shrugs. "What are you watching?"

I tell her about Aidan Wallace with his goofy ears and his choice to come so close to death on the regular. We watch for a few minutes.

"Guy's gotta be certifiable," she says. "Otherwise, how could you possibly do that? Either that or his brain is wired not to feel fear."

"Eh, maybe," I say. "Or maybe not. Maybe he just accepts the imminent possibility of death, and carries on."

By the end of my infusion, I'm grateful that Chloe is there

to drive me home. She parks in front of my building and walks with me all the way to my bedroom.

"So have you thought anymore about the vlog? And the road trip?"

I have. I'm still not sure it's the right thing to do, but it feels like the only thing to do. "I need to talk to my mother, Clo."

"Well, get on with it!"

I relax into my mattress—the best, most perfect mattress in the entire Jordan's Furniture showroom, firm underneath with a plush pillow top; a splurge purchase from the first brain tumor—and close my eyes. The darkness spins behind my lids.

"I will. Just give me a minute."

16.

BACON IS THE FIRST THING I REGISTER THE next morning.

"Good morning, my love." Mom's flipping omelets while the bacon sizzles on the other burner.

"Morning." I take a seat at the kitchen island.

Mom frowns. "You all right?"

I can't feel the toxins coursing through me after yesterday's session, but I know they're in there. I've already done a mental checklist of my body, starting at the top. My head feels okay. It'll throb later, but that's par for the course. My vision is mostly normal, just the one slight dark spot on the periphery. Even my back feels pretty good. I'm fine.

It's the thoughts pinging around in my head—the trial, the vlog, a road trip to a cryopreservation facility I haven't even mentioned yet to my mother—that are making me feel queasy. Not the chemo.

"Fine. Just sleepy."

She brightens. "Eggs?"

We eat together in silence. Liam's already gone, left for school with a kid on the third floor who is two years older and therefore approved for walking the four blocks without a parent. It's nice to have some quiet time with Mom in the morning. Usually I'm out the door while she and Liam are still tearing around the apartment trying to collect his fill-in-the-blank: homework, soccer cleats, lunchbox, show-and-tell items, library books.

I take a small bite of omelet, testing the texture on my tongue to assess whether it's going to stay down. It seems fine, so I eat a more generous forkload. Mom watches, satisfied. Then she clears her throat in a weird way that makes me look up at her.

"What?" I ask.

"Astrid, have you talked to your dad lately?"

I try to recall the last time I called Dad at the Ranch. A few weeks, at least. Maybe a month. It's not that I don't want to talk to my father; it's just that his life is so far removed from mine these days that it's hard to convey anything over the phone.

"Not *that* lately, no. If he would just get a cell phone like a normal human being, I could text him."

"Can you please call him?"

"What's your hurry?" Mom doesn't usually micromanage my relationship with Dad, but I sense some urgency in her tone.

She scoops a last mouthful of omelet off her plate. "He

needs to know about the clinical trial. He's still—we're both still your legal guardians. So . . ."

"So he needs to give his permission for me to participate? That's what you're saying?"

Mom swallows and nods. "Exactly. And I'd talk to him about it myself, but I think—I think it'll be better coming from you."

I push the rest of my breakfast away. It doesn't taste great, all of a sudden. "Can I go to school now, please?"

"You sure you're up for it? I assumed you'd stay home today."

"I want to go. Really."

"If you're sure. Get your butt up and moving, then. I'll drop you."

I feel fine all morning, but by third period, when I'm in Dahlmann's class again, wooziness starts to settle in around me, like a storm brewing. At first it comes in little hints, but then it hits full force. My head starts clouding over, until I can't think straight through the haze of dull pounding. My spine tingles. As we pack up our stuff after the bell, I take a few deep breaths.

Mohit touches my arm from behind. "You all right?"

I nod. "Fading a little."

My stomach is churning, too, and my mouth is starting to feel dry. He offers me his arm, and while we head to the cafeteria I lean on it, trying to be subtle about it so my class-mates won't get all whatever over me. Maybe some food will help.

Mo gets me lunch while I wait at a table in the corner. He returns quickly with a tray: slice of pizza, Granny Smith apple, water.

"Good?" he asks. His face is lined with anxiety.

I force a smile. "Thanks. I'm okay."

"I'm going to get my own food. I'll be right back. Don't go anywhere."

I wait until he's disappeared into the crowd before resting my head in my hands over the tray. The apple is spinning. I blink and breathe, but it's still spinning. Then it's like the whole tray is tilting away from me. I reach for it, swiping my hand toward the bottle of water, but all I succeed in doing is knocking the whole thing to the floor with a huge clatter.

Now I need water. It's all I can think about. My class-mates are glancing over their shoulders at me—Cancer Girl just spilled all her food—but I don't care. My mouth is on fire, and the bottle of water is rolling under the tables away and away and away from me.

I move my body toward the water cooler in the corner. I think so, anyway. I think I'm moving that way. Everything feels hot and clouded. Blackness pools at the edges of my vision and then creeps in farther. Noise like radio static fills my ears. And that's it.

17.

"WHY DIDN'T YOU SAY ANYTHING AT BREAK-fast?" Mom is hovering over me. Her chipper mood from this morning has evaporated, and she's returned easily to her stasis of motherly worry.

"I felt fine until lunch," I croak. My eyes sting as I force them open. As soon as the room comes into full view, my stomach churns and I grab for the trash bin next to my bed and dump my head in it. Whatever's left in me—not a lot, mostly just sour stomach bile—comes up abruptly.

Mohit strokes my hair and hands me a tissue.

I take a long sip of water, letting it cool my throat, which still feels like it's on fire. Then Mom puts her hand on my forehead for what I'm sure is the umpteenth time since she picked me up. "You feel warm."

"I don't think I have the flu, Mom. You can stop worrying about my temp."

She grabs the empty water glass and a balled-up washcloth from next to my bed, and steps toward the door. "I'll put some soup on. Mohit, you're welcome to stay for dinner. Obviously."

"Thanks, but I've got an uncle in town. Pretty sure I have to be home."

With Mom gone, I resettle myself on the pillows and motion for Mo to get comfortable.

"I really did feel fine to go to school."

He shrugs. "Eh, so you were overconfident. It's sort of par for the course for you."

I whack him on the arm. "Hey, Mo?" I take a breath, hesitating for a moment. He looks at me expectantly. "Where have you been lately?"

"When?"

"You know when. Just in general. You've been MIA. You keep saying you have stuff to take care of."

He crosses his arms behind his head, and I can see the wheels turning in his brain, like he's trying to decide how honest to be. Which is weird because, if anything, Mo normally errs on the side of being Mr. Candor.

"What?" I prod. I'm starting to get nervous.

"Well, I wasn't going to say anything, but—"

"Just spill it. You're freaking me out."

"It's nothing bad. It's just . . . I was auditioning for a jazz quartet. At MIT."

"Like a college jazz quartet?"

He lights up a little bit and I can see how excited he is, now that he's not hiding this thing from me anymore.

"It's two undergraduates and a grad student, and they're looking for an alto. One of them saw our spring concert last year and thought of me. Anyway, I auditioned, then had callbacks, and they want me to join."

"Wow, Mo. That's amazing. Why didn't you say anything?"

"I don't know. At first I didn't know if they'd offer me the spot. And also, they rehearse a lot on the weekends. And at least one evening a week as well. It's a lot of time."

"Okay."

"Okay, so, it's a lot of time away from you."

There it is. Time. Time we don't have. Time we can't waste.

"What is time, though?" I ask, stroking an imaginary goatee. "Time is but a social construct."

"Time is everything. I promised you I was all in. With you. I want to be all in."

"And I want you to be in the MIT jazz quartet. When will you perform with them?"

"Spring. They're playing at the Regattabar."

"The Regattabar? Seriously?"

"I mean, just opening for another group, but yeah."

He took me there once to see a band he liked, back when we'd just met and I'd told him I didn't *get* jazz, which was the kiss of death because he dragged me from jazz show to jazz show until I surrendered. I still don't really get jazz. But I get Mo when he's listening to it, the way his face softens around the edges and his eyes flutter closed just three-quarters, like he's so relaxed he can't even hold his eyelids completely open or completely shut.

I picture him onstage at the Regattabar, picture myself in the crowd, his eyes on me as he plays. Spring. Will I still be around in the spring?

"You have to do the jazz quartet. So I can come see you play at the Regattabar in the spring."

Mo looks at me for what feels like a long time. At last, he nods. "Okay. I'll do it, then. And you'll come see me at the Regattabar."

Now I understand that we're both going to start telling each other lies we hope will turn out to be true.

"I want to talk to you about something," I say.

My head still pounds a dull drumbeat of pain. I know my body. I know this isn't going to turn around, not this time, no matter how much magic Mom and Dr. Klein throw at me. No matter how much Mohit loves me.

"Chloe thinks we can raise the money for cryopreservation online."

I watch Mo tense up. He blinks at me. "So you're saying . . . what?"

"I want to see more Regattabar gigs. I want to see you get famous. I don't want to miss everything."

"And you think cryopreservation is the way to—what? Stave off death? It isn't, Astrid. That's not how it works. The clinical trial is a better chance at that."

"I'm not talking about the trial. I'm talking about . . .

beyond the trial. We don't know how this might work, one day. And you said you would try anything to see me again. Didn't you mean it?"

Mo rubs a hand over his face, then through his hair. He stares off into the middle distance beyond my head. "You know I'd keep you here forever if I had that power. Of course I would. I just worry . . ." He trails off.

"What? What are you worried about? What's the harm in taking this chance, even if the chance is so slim?"

"I worry that you'll put all your stock in it. That you won't fight the real fight. The one happening in this actual lifetime."

I've never particularly liked the battle metaphor for cancer, at least not since I got cancer myself. It's like there are two kinds of cancer patients: the fighters and the pushovers. And it's so obvious to everyone that the pushovers are the losers, and the fighters are the ones deserving of respect. They're the ones dying the noble deaths—because they do still die, of course; it's not like you can actually outsmart cancer just by wishing you could. But the pushovers, the ones who say, "This is it for me, and I accept that," they take the blame for their own mortality. As if, if we'd only hoped a little harder, begged the universe a little louder, we could've turned the tide of our own eventuality, but we didn't, and so we don't. Death is our own fault.

"My illness has a mind of its own, Mo. I don't own it. I don't control it. It does what it wants. So shouldn't I get to do what I want, too?"

Now it's Mohit who's quiet for a long time. Finally, he sighs softly. "I hear you. I do." His eyes, when he looks at me, are dark, watery oases. "So, then, what next?"

"According to Chloe, we make a vlog."

"What's a vlog?"

18.

THE APARTMENT IS QUIET ON SUNDAY MORNING.
I wander to the kitchen, looking for Mom, but it's empty.
There's a note stuck to the fridge.

A—I'm going to a birth, didn't want to wake you. L will
be at soccer and then Kieran's house until I'm done. Hope you
are feeling well. Page me if you need me. Loves.

A birth. I wonder how much longer Mom will be willing
to keep taking on-call shifts at the birthing center. Last time
I was sick, they moved her to just business hours—she'd see
patients at the office and follow their care, but she didn't
take on-call shifts or attend any births. Eventually, she went
on short-term leave to be able to take care of me full-time.
Her colleagues gave her their vacation time, days and days of
it, so she could still take a paycheck. She was grateful for it,
but I know how much she missed the actual birthing part of
midwifery, the part she always called the pot of gold at the

end of the nine-month rainbow. My mother loves helping other women have babies, says it's the best thing in the world after having them herself. But being on call is grueling and unpredictable, and I know she won't be able to do it forever. At least not while I'm still around.

I feel like myself again today, just vaguely depleted, like my gas tank is lower than it used to be and, no matter what, I can't get it back to full again. I pour myself a bowl of Special K and take in the quiet of the whole apartment while I eat. This is another one of those moments I'd like to capture in an app. Once you get really sick, people don't leave you alone. It's almost never quiet. In the hospital, obviously, you're getting poked and prodded and woken up at all hours. There's beeping and buzzing throughout the night, never quiet. But even at home, there's always clanging in the kitchen, Mrs. Parikh or a neighbor cooking something for us, or Mom's best friend, Thea, ordering takeout and talking to her not quite quietly enough.

Home right now feels different. I remember when my father left, it was like this, too. It was like the tenor of the place shifted, and things got quiet and too empty, and Mom said to me one day, "We should have a space of our own, shouldn't we?" We were in a house back then, of course, the one in the country, and that was part of the reason we moved. I mean, there was the money part, but it was also because of the sounds. I was twelve. Liam was only four. We've been in this apartment ever since. Only now, when it's quiet, it's on our own terms, a peaceful quiet, not the kind left behind when someone you love disappears.

I wonder if Mom and Liam will move again.

After breakfast, I get back in bed with a mug of green tea. Getting back in bed on a Sunday without feeling guilty about it is one of the rare perks of being Cancer Girl, and hell if I'm going to pass it up. I snuggle down into my comforter. For another moment, while I let the steam from the tea warm my chin and cheeks, I enjoy the silence and wonder how Mom's birth is going. Is the baby here yet? (Probably not, or I would've gotten a text.) When I was little I used to want to be a midwife just like her. I thought it was pretty fascinating, the idea that you could be there at the very moment when someone else's life starts. Now it makes me happy that after I'm gone, once she's gotten back to herself enough to return to work, she'll be surrounded most days by new lives starting, instead of ending.

I call Chloe.

"Are you dying or something?" she mutters sleepily. "Because otherwise there's no good reason to be calling me this early on a Sunday."

"It's after ten."

"Don't judge." I hear Chloe stretching on the other side of the phone. "How are you feeling?"

"Better today. Did everyone gossip about my impending death for the rest of the day on Friday?"

"Only for like an hour. Lucky for you, at some point between fifth and sixth periods, Emma Lightfoot and Dylan

Chung had a massive fight in the first-floor entryway and broke up in front of at least fifty very interested witnesses, so by the end of the day your nosedive for the water cooler was forgotten."

"Thanks, Emma and Dylan. I always knew I could count on you." Emma Lightfoot and Dylan Chung are forever on and off again. It's actually fairly boring, but for some reason my classmates find it an endlessly worthwhile source of entertainment.

"Seriously though," Chloe says. "No one was gossiping. They were just concerned."

The fact that my classmates might have shifted from being intrigued by my illness to being just plain worried is, for some reason, more alarming to me than the whole passing-out-in-the-cafeteria thing to begin with.

I swallow the lump in my throat. "I want to go to Arizona. I have to see this place before I invest in my future as a science experiment. So let's make this vlog."

I can hear Chloe getting out of bed, the blankets around her rustling as she shifts into immediate action. "Say no more. I'm on it. I'll be over in an hour. Call your boyfriend—I'm going to need a key grip."

"Do you even know what a key grip does?"

"Astrid, just call Mo."

The lighting in my bedroom isn't quite to Chloe's taste, so she drags in a couple of extra standing lamps from the living room. Mohit perches on the bed, looking mildly skeptical about this whole undertaking.

"Your room should be tidy but not sterile," Clo says, looking around at my scattered clothes and the desk piled with notebooks and disorganized heaps of scrap paper.

"Mohit, can you fix that?" Chloe nods toward the unmade bed. "Make yourself useful, at least." When Chloe gets it in her head to do something, a project, we all know better than to question her directives. Mo feels it, too, I can tell. He gets up to do what she tells him.

Chloe tidies the desk, hides a few random sweatshirts in the closet. Then she positions my desk chair in front of the bed and gestures for me to sit.

"I'm going to look terrible. Can I please put some more makeup on?" I'm wearing moisturizer, mascara, and the tiniest bit of blush. I definitely look like I haven't slept in years.

"First of all, you're beautiful. Second of all, you have cancer, remember?"

"I do remember that, yes."

"So you can't look like you just stepped off a runway. You're asking for strangers' money."

I sigh. She's probably right.

"Besides, like I said, you look hot. Mo, doesn't she look hot?"

"She always looks hot," Mohit says absently from the corner where he's picking up dirty laundry off the floor and shoving it into my closet. Still making up for telling me he doesn't like my blue hair, I guess. I'll take it.

Chloe peers through the lens of her camera and adjusts the focus.

"Where'd you get the camera, Clo?"

"Mom A, obviously. I seriously cannot break it, or she will kill me." Annalisa is an actual photographer with a studio of her own. She has many cameras, and I'm guessing this is one of the cheapest of the bunch, but still probably not something we want to have to replace.

"All right, so, remember," Chloe says. "You're very charming. You're very smart. You had a bright future ahead of you. Now you're dying of cancer."

The words hang in the air around us. I glance at Mo, who averts his eyes toward the ceiling.

Even Chloe's face clouds over. "Sorry," she says quietly.

I don't say anything, and the room stays silent and still for a long moment. It's like we've been going and going and have only now stopped to acknowledge the madness around us. Because Chloe's not wrong. I am dying of cancer. We are making a video to explain that to a bunch of strangers. I am asking them to give me their money in exchange for a chance—a tiny, slim, almost nonexistent chance—at some kind of resurrection. It makes no sense at all when you actually pause to think about it.

Which, I guess, is why I don't want to pause anymore.

19.

HI, EVERYONE. SO THIS IS AWKWARD. UM,
yeah, hi. My name is Astrid Ayeroff. Who's named Astrid, right? No
one else I know, except the Scandinavian woman who wrote Pippi
Longstocking *in, like, the 1940s.*

Anyway, my name is Astrid. I'm sixteen years old. I'm a junior in
high school and, yeah, I have a high-grade astrocytoma, which is a
tumor in my brain. Which means, in the short term, I'm dying. I
know this is going to sound totally crazy, but I'm hoping you can help
me, in the long term, one day, wake up again.

20.

I GET A TEXT FROM MOM AROUND FOUR:
*Could be a long night over here. L staying at K's. Feeling OK? Love
you.* But then a few hours later, shortly after I've had a pizza
with onions and peppers delivered—large, because I know
Mom'll need something to reheat whenever she gets home—I
hear keys in the door.

"Wasn't expecting to see you until tomorrow," I say as
Mom dumps her bag in the front hall—doesn't even bother
to hang her coat, either—and slumps down next to me on
the couch. Her face is pale, exhausted, like I remember her
looking after the long, half-sleepless nights on the recliner
next to my bed when I was admitted to the hospital last time
around. She rubs her eyes hard enough that it looks like she
might displace them from their sockets.

"Things kicked into gear shortly after I texted you. Baby
was born around six." Mom rests her head on my shoulder.
"You all right?"

I nod. "What was it?"

"What was what?" Mom's eyes are closed. She breathes heavily, deep-inhaling through her nose and long-exhaling through her mouth.

"The baby, duh."

"Oh. Baby girl. Full head of hair. Born in the water."

"Like Liam." Liam was born in the water, at home in the middle of a freak April snowstorm that closed school for three days. It didn't really matter about the snow; my mother had been planning to have him at home anyway, in a blow-up birthing pool she'd rented from a hippie website. She worked in a hospital, but she'd had a homebirth with me and insisted on having one with Liam, too, even though all signs pointed toward him being a giant baby. We were in the country house then, in the woods. It was dark except for the light coming off the moon and the snow. And quiet, except for the sound of my mother's breath and my father's barked, anxious questions for the midwife—Mom's favorite colleague, stuck at her own house in the snow—over speakerphone. I was eight, and I spent the night in my bedroom with the door cracked, awake and listening.

Liam was born just before sunrise. Mom had called my name a moment before, and I'd gone to the side of the pool. I watched her arch her back and tip her head toward the ceiling, and then there was Liam, swimming under her.

He's eight now, the age I was then. I wonder if he'll remember my death as clearly as I remember his birth.

"Yes, like Liam. Only this baby didn't weigh ten ever-loving pounds, fortunately for her mother." Mom yawns. "Is there food?"

She goes into the kitchen and I hear her reheating a slice of pizza in the toaster oven. When she returns to the couch next to me, I take in her face while she isn't paying attention. She closes her eyes, focusing—as she does—on exactly what she's doing in this present moment: chewing pizza, in this case. The look on her face, so much pleasure for one slice of reheated veggie, makes me dread the conversation we're about to have.

"Hey, Mom? Can I talk to you about something?"

"Always."

I hesitate again, but then I dive in. I tell her about Carl Vanderwalk at the symposium, and about the American Institute for Cryonics Research and their vision of a future where death is just one more thing that happens. She listens, her face immobile, until I'm done.

"Astrid . . ." She halts after my name. It floats in the air.

I want to say something to fill the space, but as with Mohit, I know better. I should just give her the silence.

"Astrid," she repeats after a moment. "We're not *there*, yet."

"What is 'there,' Mom?" I know what she means. I don't know why I want to force her to say it out loud.

"You're not . . . We're not talking about the—the end."

She won't say it. She won't say "death."

"We are, Mom. I am."

"I'm not, though." Her voice catches. I reach for her hand and squeeze it, something I never do, and she lets me.

"I didn't pass out in school because I had the flu or something," I say.

"I know that." She's speaking very softly. "But the chemo will do what it's supposed to do."

"I'm going to die this time." I didn't notice her starting to cry, but now I see that her face is soaked. She doesn't wipe any of the tears away. "I'm sorry, Mom. I'm sorry to leave you."

She lets out a sob, then quickly reins it back in, a hand to her mouth. "*I'm* sorry, Astrid. You shouldn't see your mother like this."

"Mom, it's not your fault. You just got a dud."

Mom laughs, that garbled, it's-totally-not-funny-but-we're-going-to-laugh-anyway-because-what-the-hell-else-are-we-supposed-to-do kind of laugh. Then she pulls herself together.

"Astrid." She shakes her head, her face turning serious all of a sudden. "You have a place in a clinical trial for pediatric brain cancer—basically one of the most promising *ever*, according to Dr. Klein. We kicked this once already. We can kick it again."

"Mom—"

"No, listen to me. I'm your mother. I'm not letting you just give up on your life."

"I'm not giving up, Mom. I'm doing the trial, aren't I?" The voice in the back of my head keeps asking me why: Why spend my last however many good months seeing doctors and lab technicians and trying to stay *very still* in the dark tube of an MRI machine? But I don't say that thought out loud to Mom.

"I'm not giving up," I repeat. "But I want to explore this. As an option, if it comes to that."

Mom starts to protest again, but I put my hand up to stop her.

"Come on. You're an intelligent human being. You're a medical professional. You know no treatment is guaranteed to work."

She sits back against the couch cushions. Her eyes sparkle with just a hint of moisture. I expect her to say something, to keep pushing me, but she's quiet.

I go on. "Even if cryopreservation doesn't work for, like, a hundred years and everyone I know is dead by then—or even if it *never* works and my body just sits in a freezer for eternity—I might as well be part of science. I can't be part of science if I'm rotting in the ground."

She remains quiet for a long time. Like, a long time. Almost more time than I can handle. "And here I was, thinking we'd keep you on the mantel," she says finally, a wry half-smile creeping over her face.

"That's great, Mother. I'm glad you've got a plan."

Mom takes a long, hard breath, then lets it out. "Oh, Astrid, my girl."

She leans into me, putting her head in my lap and pulling her legs up onto the couch. I stroke her hair, all soft auburn curls that I didn't inherit, although she's got way more gray hairs now than she did a couple of years ago.

"You don't understand."

"Don't understand what?"

"What it is to have a child."

"Please, Mom."

"I'm serious. You have no idea what it means to be a parent. There's nothing, Astrid—"

She cuts herself off. I watch the top of her head, resting in my lap. Her body rises and falls with her breath, and I twist my fingers in her curls.

"There was a moment, a few weeks after you were born, when I was up with you in the middle of the night. Did I ever tell you this story?"

I shake my head. She smiles, picturing whatever she's picturing. Baby Astrid, I guess.

"I was awake with you, not because you were crying but because you *weren't* crying. You were sleeping, perfectly fine. But there I was, wide awake, checking to see if you were breathing. I remember that moment of all the times I was up with you in the middle of the night because it was the first time I realized that I was never going to be free from worry again."

"See, this is why I'm glad I'm not having kids."

"Oh, cut it out."

"Mom, seriously. I don't want you to spend your life worrying about me."

"It's not a choice! It's life. It's biology. My point is just that I'm never going to stop trying to keep you on this earth. Even if I have to hover over you and watch you take every breath. So no, Astrid, I'm not going to entertain the notion of your body in a deep freeze. And you don't get to tell me that

I have to accept the end of your life. I'm your mother, and it doesn't work that way."

But I'm *me*, I think. Still, I decide to leave it be.

Later, with my mother snoring down the hall, I open my email and start a new message.

Dear Dr. Fitzspelt:

It was a pleasure to meet your colleague, Dr. Carl Vanderwalk, at the neuroscience symposium a couple of months ago. When we met, I mentioned that I am dying. That's still true. I don't know for sure whether or not I want to pursue cryopreservation, but I would like to know more.

Dr. Vanderwalk suggested I contact you. If you'll have me, I'd like to come to Arizona to see your facilities. Do you give tours?

Thank you for your time.

Sincerely,
Astrid Ayeroff

I watch the video one more time on my phone. I can barely bring myself to look at my on-screen face: the shock of stringy hair, perpetually bed-headed because even though I've had it short twice now, I still haven't learned how to do anything useful with it except turn it blue. And the dark circles under my eyes, a sharper angle to my jaw—small signs of illness creeping in that probably no one but me notices yet.

Well, I'm sure my mother notices. My mother notices everything. There's a knot in the pit of my stomach when I think about how she'll react when she sees this.

On-Screen Astrid looks straight at the camera and introduces herself. Then there's the wind-up, and the pitch.

My hope is to freeze my body through cryopreservation. This is a new and rapidly evolving science in which bodies are preserved at the time of death. The goal is to be able to wake people up one day. Scientists don't know what will be possible decades from now. I don't know either. I'm asking you, friends of the internet, to help me find out.

Here's the thing: I have to come up with around $31,000 to cryopreserve myself. Some of that will cover the cost of a trip to Arizona, to visit the cryopreservation lab and learn more about the process. The rest would go toward the preservation itself. It's a big investment, and I normally wouldn't do this—make my story public, and ask for help from strangers. But my mom is raising me and my little brother on her own, and she's already got a kid with cancer on her hands, so I really don't want to be any larger of a burden on her than I already am. So I'm asking. If you're interested in this future science—which I realize sounds totally bananas—or you *just feel inclined to donate to The Association of Random Freaks on the Internet Who Believe Death Might Not Be the End of Life, current membership: one, now's your chance.*

On-Screen Astrid pauses again, and a crack appears in her stoic facade. I remember this moment, the emotion of it catching me off guard. I wanted to yell at Chloe to turn the camera off, but I bit my lip instead, and pushed back the tears that threatened to humiliate me in front of the people of the internet.

Seriously. Thank you.

My stomach floods with anxiety, thinking about people—strangers and, maybe worse, *nonstrangers*—watching this. Kids at school. Neighbors. Mohit's parents, his sister in business school. My mother.

Mom doesn't have to like this, but she can't stop me from asking questions.

I text Chloe, and tell her I'm ready to go live.

21.

Things I'll miss when I'm dead (a partial list, continued):
The sound of my mother telling my brother a bedtime story
   in the other room when they think I can't hear them
Scrambled eggs
Eggs over easy
Eggs of all kinds, really
Chloe bossing me around
The internet, maybe

22.

THE PLANET DOESN'T STOP ROTATING WHEN

I ask the internet for help bringing me back from the dead. Mostly, no one pays any attention at all. The views tick up gradually—fifteen, then twenty. A few donations come in, mostly from people I know, classmates and teachers. A week goes by and, basically, nothing much happens. I'm beginning to wonder if Chloe was wrong: there are too many interesting things on the internet; no one cares about my story.

It's unseasonably warm on Wednesday, but pouring rain. As usual, Mohit rushes off to MIT the minute the last bell rings, and Chloe has math team, so I get the bus home by myself to avoid the downpour. In our empty apartment, I take a Coke from the fridge and slouch at the kitchen table, my phone in front of me. Mom reminded me for the umpteenth time this morning as she was leaving the house, "Please, Astrid, for the love of god, call your father." I may as well get it over with.

The phone rings through to the main lodge at the Ranch, as I know it will. A young woman answers. When I tell her who's calling, her tone turns saccharine, and she earnestly informs me, "Your dad has been so worried. He'll be grateful to hear from you." She tells me she'll get the message to him right away, and he'll call back.

I wait, staring out the kitchen window at the street below. Five minutes later, the phone vibrates against the table.

"Astrid, my darling girl." He's out of breath, as though he's run from his tiny house to the lodge, eager to speak to his dying kid.

"Hi, Dad."

"How are you?"

"I'm fine. How are you? And . . . Suzanne?" *She's barely that much older than Astrid*, I remember Mom saying to her friend Thea, several glasses of wine in, when they thought I wasn't listening. To be totally fair, that was a touch hyperbolic of her. Suzanne may not be as old as Dad, but she's definitely old enough to be legally wed.

"We're . . ." My father hesitates for a moment. "Well, we're all right. I don't want to talk about us. Astrid, are you feeling run-down? How's your energy?"

Outside, the bus pulls up, number 77, the same one I took home earlier. I hear the wheels exhale toward the ground—it's a kneeling bus—and then the wheelchair ramp unfolding. An older woman in an electric wheelchair rolls herself down to the sidewalk and buzzes away down the street, her plume of white hair covered by a plastic shopping bag fashioned into a shower cap.

"I'm fine, really, Dad."

He's quiet for a moment, then clears his throat. "Astrid, you know, I've said this to your mother, and I . . . I really wish you would both take me more seriously when I say that the way you live your lives is not conducive to . . . healing."

If my eyes could roll all the way back in my head, they would. He barrels on, not waiting for a response—which is good, because I have none.

"You know, I mean, the amount of toxins you're living with, both physically and psychopharmacologically, you know . . . they wear on the mind and body. And the brain. Your brain is directly responding to what you expose it to. And if you're not exposing it to what it needs to heal, it's just . . . Well, it's a magnet for atrophy and disease."

He stops there. I don't say anything. "Astrid? Are you still there?"

"I'm here, Dad."

"I'm not saying I blame you and your mother for your illness, obviously . . ."

Right.

"What I'm saying is just that, you know, you're relying on Western medicine, chemotherapy—all these drugs—to fix it, but aren't you just reinforcing the toxic environment that bred the tumor in the first place?"

I tug at the shade on the kitchen window and bite the side of my cheek. "My tumor was *bred* when glial cells called astrocytes in my brain began to multiply out of control, rather than following the standard cellular pattern of growth, division, and death. It's science, Dad. It's not because our couch gives off VOCs."

"VOCs are one thing, Astrid. I'm talking about much more than that."

"Okay."

"I didn't mean to upset you."

"You're not upsetting me, Dad. I just thought I should tell you I got a place in a clinical trial. That's why I'm calling."

I wonder if there are others sitting around him in the lodge, listening to his end of the conversation—or even my end, if I'm on speakerphone or something, being broadcast to his entire community. I wonder if Suzanne is listening.

"So more drugs, then."

"The trial is intended to boost my immune system to fight the cancer. They're testing drugs that could block the proteins that normally stop the immune response."

"Boost your immune system?" I hear him register this, like I'm suddenly speaking a language he understands. "Surely you can boost your immune response through natural approaches, though. Are more drugs really necessary?"

"Dad, you can't just echinacea your way through cancer."

"Of course. I know that. And you know more about this than I do. But, Astrid, I'm just saying, it's not too late for you to cleanse your body and mind and put yourself in a better position for healing. Why don't you come see me out here, and bring—what's his name? You still have that same boyfriend?"

"Mohit."

"Yes, yes, Mo-heat."

I hate the way my father mispronounces Mo's name, deliberately, as though *he's* the one saying it correctly.

"Mo-heat must understand and appreciate the power of alternative sources of healing."

My eyes, once again, are desperate to roll as far back into my head as humanly possible. "Because he's Indian, you mean? His father is a phlebotomist, Dad."

"Well, anyway. I don't want to fight with you about this. I love you, Astrid."

"Mom needs you to sign some papers for this clinical trial. I have to have both guardians' permission."

"I'm not going to stand in your way, Astrid. I just think there are other options."

I sigh. "Okay. Thanks. I have to go, Dad."

"Think about coming to visit. All right? Astrid?"

I let the shade snap all the way back up to the top of the window frame. "Fine. We'll think about it. I have to go."

"Take care, my darling. I love you—you know that."

"Mmm. Bye."

23.

I HAVE TO WATCH TWO EPISODES OF *PLANET*
Earth on the Discovery Channel to dispel my irritation toward
my father, but by the time I hear Mom and Liam clamber into
the front hall two hours later, I've actually managed to get
some work done on my problem set for Dahlmann. Mom's
footsteps pound down the hall toward my room, and then
without warning the door is thrown wide open with what can
only be described as a maternal hurricane.

"Are you kidding me, Astrid? Seriously?" Her face is
flushed.

"Mom, what the hell!"

"I told you we weren't doing this cryo-whatever-nonsense.
I told you no. You're in this trial. That's our next move. Period, end of story, finished. And you're putting this on the
internet! Telling people we need money because I'm a single
mother? Are you kidding me right now, Astrid Ayeroff? You
know how I found out about this?"

I don't, and I'm kind of wondering, but I'm not sure I

want to know. Mom doesn't give me a chance to answer her anyway.

"*Liam* saw it," she goes on. "Your eight-year-old brother. And you know how he saw it? Because some kid in his class has an older brother who goes to school with you, so now word has trickled down from the high school to his class, and they all know he has a sister with cancer who's 'vlogging' about how she's going to freeze herself after she dies."

Her mouth curls around the word "vlogging," like that bastardized use of the English language is among the worst of my offenses.

"So he asks me about it, and of course I—your mother—have no idea! Which is how I found myself watching that video of you on YouTube. And I'm apparently the last person in the neighborhood who knows about it."

She finally pauses to take a breath. Of all the possible eventualities of putting that video on the internet, Liam seeing it is one I did not think of. Which was stupid. Liam ordered all his own Christmas presents off Amazon when he was six—wooden trains, action figures, and a junior fashion designer sketchbook with colored pencils and fabric swatches showed up at the door in a succession of Prime boxes until Mom finally figured out that she'd saved her credit card information in there—so I shouldn't be surprised that he knows how to navigate YouTube. Still, I didn't consider that he'd see the video. That might be the worst outcome of this whole thing.

"Mom." I sigh. "Okay. I'm sorry."

"I explicitly told you that we weren't entertaining this, didn't I?"

"Technically you didn't, exactly. You—"

The door behind Mom opens and Liam's little face appears. "Are you guys fighting about that video?" He doesn't look particularly traumatized, just mildly concerned.

"No," we both say at the same time.

"I'm sorry, baby," Mom says, picking him up even though he's way too big to be picked up. She cuddles him and kisses his brown curls. "I'm sorry. I got upset for a minute."

"It's nothing, kid," I say. "I just made Mom a little bit mad. It happens."

He buries his face in her shoulder, then looks up. "Can we get Thai food for dinner?"

"Sure," Mom says. "Can you do me a favor? Get the menu out and decide what you want."

"I want pad thai."

"Can you go to the kitchen and look at the menu anyway, just for a minute? And then I'll call?"

Liam frowns and gives Mom his best I'm-not-buying-it look, but when she puts him down, he scampers off toward the kitchen. Mom watches him go, then looks back up at me.

"You were saying," she says.

"I think I was saying I'm sorry."

"Uh-huh."

"But, Mom, you didn't say I *couldn't* even learn about cryo-preservation. The whole point of the video is so I can explore it, and you don't have to worry about it because you won't need to give me the money for any of it. I just want to go visit the place, okay? As a start, to see the facility and talk to the people. Learn more."

"Why didn't you tell me that?"

"I tried, but you went all mom-with-a-dying-kid on me."

She doesn't respond, just stands there looking almost petulant. I feel like we're having a strange reversal of traditional roles.

"I talked to Dad," I add. "He's fine with the trial. He still thinks I have cancer because we have a television or whatever."

"Your father is a special human being." Mom rolls her eyes. "Astrid, I don't know. This all seems . . . premature."

"It's not. And, Mom? I know you made me and all that, and I'm not saying that doesn't count for anything. But, like, don't I get a say in the rest of my life? And/or death?"

The color drains from her face. She looks exhausted.

"Just a visit?" I prod.

Finally, Mom sighs and turns toward the door. "Liam! Bring the menu in here, baby!" She looks back at me. "Maybe."

24

THE EMAIL COMES TWO DAYS LATER:

Dear Ms. Ayeroff:

My sincere apologies for my delayed reply. My
assistant alerted me to your message, but I confess,
my inbox sometimes gets away from me. I hope you'll
forgive me. My deepest sympathies, too, that you find
yourself nearing the end of your present life. I can
only imagine the heartache you and your family are
experiencing, to receive a diagnosis like that at such
a tender age.

We most certainly would welcome you to the
American Institute for Cryonics Research for a tour.
I would be delighted to show you around myself, and
to answer any questions you might have. I hope the
possibility of the cryopreservation process may

provide some comfort to you, some hope for a future beyond the limited one you have been shown by your doctors. That hope is our gift to you and yours, should you wish to accept it.

I have copied my assistant on this email. Please let us know when you would like to visit.

Best wishes,
Dr. A. R. Fitzspelt

25.

MRS. PARIKH LOOKS SURPRISED TO SEE ME
when I ring their bell on Sunday morning. "Astrid. Hi, dear."
A gust of warm air blows out the front door, bringing the
familiar smell of Mo's house, with its different cleaning sup-
plies and spices. Mrs. Parikh frowns. "Everything okay?
Come on in."

When I step into the vestibule and take my shoes off—
Parikh house rules—I can hear Mo's horn coming from upstairs, muffled by the floor between us. I hate to interrupt his
rehearsal, but I need to talk to him, and he's been taking off
so quickly after school that I feel like I barely see him anymore.

"He's up there, as usual. I guess you can tell. Go on up.
You're . . ." Mrs. Parikh hesitates. "Are you okay to go up the
stairs on your own?"

"Yes, thanks." I give her a smile and she looks relieved,
not because she wouldn't want to help me up the stairs—
she's one of the nicest moms I know—but probably because
she didn't want to offend me by trying.

I bang on Mo's door once, but the playing doesn't stop, so I go right in. He's in his usual corner, by the window, back to the door. He doesn't even notice my presence when I slink over and land on his desk chair.

It's a piece I haven't heard before, with a low, melancholy melody. I rest my head on the back of the chair and watch him, his eyes closed but his face responding to the notes as he plays them. He leans into the music, bending forward at the knees and then back. After a moment, he hits something wrong and stops abruptly. His eyes shoot open.

"Oh shit!" He jumps when he sees me. "Gosh, Astrid! You scared me."

"Sorry. I did knock."

"Obviously I didn't hear you. Hi." He kisses me. "What are you doing here?"

I need to talk to him about our road trip to Arizona, but I don't want to dive right in. Instead I push his desk chair around in a circle. "Nothing. I just hadn't seen you in a few days."

"I saw you at school on Thursday." Ever since my post-chemo incident in the cafeteria, Mom has insisted I stay home on Fridays after my Thursday-afternoon infusions.

"I know, but that was, like, three days ago. And it was in math class. It doesn't count."

"Sorry. We rehearsed after school on Friday and then all day yesterday. These guys are so intense, man. They know everything about jazz. They talk about artists I've never even heard of, like this guy Johnny Griffin . . ." He lets his saxophone dangle from the strap around his neck and starts tapping on his phone. "He's so good."

"That's awesome, Mo." I listen for a minute, not that I'm sure what I'm listening for. I can't tell good jazz from crappy jazz, no matter how many times Mohit tries to give me some "helpful parameters for listening." It all sounds the same to me: a mishmash of disjointed sounds, with the occasional melody I can grasp. Except when Mo's playing. When Mo's playing, it's like watching the Perseids all over again, every time. Like bright light burning through the dark sky, like pure magic.

"Seriously, they name-drop these musicians and I have to pretend I know what they're talking about until I can google them."

I zone out, basking in the sound of his voice as he drones on. The words themselves blur together. He's so happy, and I miss him already, even though he's right in front of me. Maybe I won't mention the trip to Arizona, after all.

26.

THERE'S NOTHING EXCITING TO LOOK AT ON the ceiling of Dr. Klein's exam room. I've had a lot of opportunities to think about this: doctors should really put something interesting on their office ceilings. My dentist's office, for example, has a light panel on the ceiling that projects soothing scenes from nature—oceans, sunsets, et cetera. That's not bad. It'd be even better if you could read an e-book, or catch up on TV, or do, like, a word search or something. Anything. But no, here at Dr. Klein's, it's just a plain old drop ceiling, pocked with fluorescent lights. Hardly doing its part to make the experience of lying on a cold table in a paper gown more humane.

I'm not actually in a gown right now. Dr. Klein just gives me a quick once-over because she says medicine is really a tactile art; the scans and labs alone aren't enough for her. She gently probes at the nodes on my neck, shines her little light in my eyes, and watches my gaze follow her fingers. Then she asks me to sit up so she can listen to my chest and back.

"Thanks, Astrid," she says when she's done, like she always

does, as though I've done her some favor by subjecting my sick body to her care. Maybe I have, in some ways. She loves what she does. Thanks to my cancer, she gets to become a better doctor. I just get to be dead.

"So, aside from the episode at school, which I think we can chalk up to a little bit of overexertion for the day after an infusion . . ." She pauses there to give me a stern look. "Other than that, you've felt more or less okay?"

I glance at Mom, who's tapping her foot rapidly against the leg of her chair.

"Pretty much."

Dr. Klein waits, like she always does, to see if I'm going to say more.

"I've been a little more tired than usual. Like, getting out of breath a little more quickly."

She nods. "Headaches are about the same? And your vision?"

"Yeah. Well, maybe a little more haziness in my peripheral vision."

"Okay. Well, look, your scans are not bad."

"What does 'not bad' mean, exactly?" Mom asks.

"Your tumor has grown a little bit, as you probably guessed from the increased fatigue and vision loss, right?"

She looks at me, so I nod, because it's true.

"But if we're taking the view that your tumor has proved itself to be fairly aggressive already, I would say that the growth we're seeing right now is not as alarming as it could be. Growth has slowed since your last scans."

"Slowed? So the chemo is working?" Mom perks up.

"The tumor's not receding, Maxine. We have to be realistic about that. But it hasn't spread beyond the brain at this point, which is great, because it means you're still eligible for the trial. So in that respect, yes, I would say the chemo is helping."

Mom seems satisfied with that, as satisfied as she can be.

"And your side effects have been manageable?"

I shrug. The antiemetic she put me on after the first chemo session has kept me from feeling too nauseated. My hair is starting to come out in tangled tufts of brown and blue, but that much I expected. Dr. Klein carries on, explaining that she's going to outfit me with an oxygen tank I can drag around behind me.

"Come on, really?" I groan. "I'll look like a sick person."

"Only when you need it. You make the call, Astrid. But at least you'll have it, so if you want to go on a longer walk or do something more strenuous, you can, and you'll have this as an option to help you."

I think of my trip with Mo to the amusement park, and how I might've made it through the day if I could've taken some O_2 breaks, like a climber heading up Everest. If there's a trade-off, I guess, between looking like a sick person and feeling moderately more like a healthy person, I should probably take the latter.

"There's one more thing," Mom says as we're getting ready to leave. "Astrid wants to take a trip to Arizona for a few days, to visit, um, a research facility." She's careful not to mention the purpose of this particular research facility, and Dr. Klein, with the subtlest of looks in my direction, indicates that she's not going to give away the fact that I talked to her about cryopreservation long before I mentioned it to my own mother. "What do you think about . . . I mean, it'd be a lot for her, don't you think? To travel that far? And I wouldn't want her to miss any infusions."

"Sure, she'd be tired," Dr. Klein allows. Before Mom can interject, she goes on. "But I'm fine with it if you are, Maxine. It's your call. I see no medical reason why she shouldn't go at this point."

I shoot Mom a triumphant look, which is met by what I can only describe as her I-don't-like-this-but-you're-probably-going-to-get-your-way face, a favorite of mine. As we get our things together to leave, I give Dr. Klein a covert thumbs-up.

I probably shouldn't feel so excited, but I like winning, even in dubious circumstances.

27.

CHLOE AND I SPREAD THE MAPS ACROSS THE
kitchen table. She printed them off Google and taped them
together in eight-and-a-half-by-eleven sections. My mother
surveys our work skeptically.

"Look, here's the plan." I point out the route marked in a
meandering red line from Boston to Sedona, all 2,567 miles
of it. "Chloe has it all worked out so we can do it over February
vacation. It won't take us *that* long. Like, three days each
way if we do it straight. A day or two longer if we stop to
sightsee. Don't you want me to see the country while I still
can?"

Mom frowns at the maps. "There's not a closer facility for
this . . . kind of thing? Really?"

I shake my head. "This is the one, Mom. This is where
my body would be." I see her flinch at the words. "Don't you
think I should see the real thing?"

"I do, Astrid, I do. It's just a long trip for you. And a lot of
time for me to take off work, too."

I glance from Mom to Chloe and back. "Mom, see, I was thinking: you shouldn't take off work for this."

"If we fly, I might not have to." She's distracted now, tapping on her phone—probably checking flights. She makes a face. "Yikes. I guess Arizona is a popular destination in February."

"Mom, listen. What if Chloe and Mo and I did the trip together?"

"You guys can come!" Mom says. "Sure. If your parents don't mind."

"No." I sigh. "*Mom*, I mean, what if we did it as a friend trip? No parents. You wouldn't have to miss any work."

She lets out a sharp laugh.

"I'm serious. Don't you want me to have, like, a typical teenage independent travel experience?"

"So you're telling me your version of spring break is going to be a visit to a cryopreservation facility?"

"Technically, it's winter break, but yes. I mean, I'm working with a narrow set of parameters here."

"I also factored in some fun stops along the way, Maxine," Chloe says, holding up *The Top 50 Roadside Attractions*. "So it'll be less business-trip-to-see-body-freezers and more, like, tour-of-classic-Americana-with-friends-plus-confronting-your-mortality-along-the-way. Know what I mean?"

"That's great, Chloe. Thanks," Mom says dryly. She takes the book and thumbs through a few pages, an eyebrow cocked. "Astrid, I really don't think it's a good idea. What if something happens and you need emergency care? You'll be so far from home, without me. I just . . . I can't see it. Sorry."

"Mom, Dr. Klein said she saw no medical reason why I shouldn't go, remember? I think we can safely say a week on the road is not going to be the thing that kills me at this point. And if it is, lucky me."

"Oh, Astrid." Mom sighs audibly and stares at the maps. "How would you three even get there? We only have one car."

"My moms already said we could borrow the Tomato," Chloe pipes up. Chloe's mothers drive Subaru Outbacks like all the other Cambridge Ladies, but their prized possession—fired up only for special occasions like their annual summer camping trips and now languishing in the driveway because they can't decide who gets custody of it—is a red RV affectionately known as the Sundried Tomato, for obvious reasons.

Mom turns to me. "You decided to acquire a vehicle for this before even discussing it with me?"

"I mean, they said they're okay with it if you're okay with it," Chloe says quickly. "I'm not hearing a lot of 'no' these days. Divorce perk."

"And, Mom, Sedona's not that far from the Ranch, either. I could visit Dad on the way."

"Girls, I . . . come on. You're killing me here, Astrid. Seriously."

"Just one chance for an independent travel experience, Mom. That's all I'm asking."

She puts her hands on her hips, then takes one more look at the maps on the table. I can tell I've put her in a corner that she can't figure her way out of. "Oh, for heaven's sake. Fine. Okay."

28.

"THIS IS IT?" OVER LUNCH THE NEXT AFTERNOON,
Chloe scrolls through an image search of the American Institute for Cryonics Research on her phone. "I mean, it just looks like a random building in the middle of an office park. You're sure there are frozen bodies in there?"

Chloe's right. The institute is just a drab cement block with what looks like very few windows and a large, half-empty parking lot out front. It hardly screams "The future of science is here!"

"And can we come up with a better name for frozen dead bodies?" she says. "I feel like they could use better branding. Corpsicles?"

"Oh, come on." Mohit picks up his tray and piles the detritus of his lunch on top of it. "It's not exactly a joke, is it?"

Chloe and I watch him stomp off toward the busing station. Then she turns to me and rolls her eyes. "Mr. Good Humor these days, isn't he?"

"Corpsicles, though? Really?" I say.

"You have something better?"

I search my brain for something clever, but nothing surfaces. Mo comes back and sits down across from me, sulking.

Chloe takes in the vague aura of hostility radiating off Mohit and mops up the last of the ketchup on her plate with a soggy oven fry. Then she wipes her hands clean on a bunched-up napkin and stands. "Uh, well, I forgot I have something very important to do. Later."

"What's up with you?" I ask Mo when Chloe's out of earshot.

He exhales and looks at me like it's an absurd question. "You didn't think to talk to me about this road-trip idea before you and Chloe planned the whole thing and got your mom on board?"

"It's our February break. I didn't know you had so many plans."

"Well, I do have plans." He crosses his arms over his chest and lets out a huff, significant enough that a dark curl lying haphazardly across his forehead actually bounces in response.

I take a swig of water. My head feels hazy, like it's an overcast day with high humidity inside my skull, and what I need is a nap, not an argument. But that doesn't seem to be in our plans at the moment.

"What plans?"

"It's not vacation week at MIT, Astrid. Obviously."

His jazz quartet. Of course.

"I'd have to miss a week's worth of rehearsals. And we're

picking up extra hours starting in February to get ready for the Regattabar gig. It's the first week of April."

"Okay, okay. I hear you."

"You're the one who told me to do the quartet. And now you want me to bail on them."

"I don't want you to *bail* on them, I just—"

"And my parents are saying no. They say I made a commitment to this group, and I can't miss that much rehearsal. Not unless it's an emergency."

He sort of mutters that last sentence, as though he realizes that this parental loophole is probably code for "You can miss rehearsal if your girlfriend kicks it."

We sit in silence for a moment, just the white noise of the cafeteria buzzing around us. The bell sounds for fourth period.

"I have a chemistry test," I say, getting to my feet. "And I'm not moving that quickly today."

"I'll walk you there." He jumps up and offers me an elbow, which I take, even though my face is hot with frustration and I want to be able to stomp off by myself like a normal angsty teenager. I guess that's my latest casualty to cancer: the ability to express my teenage angst with as much angstiness as I feel. Which makes the feelings that much more acute.

We don't talk on the way to the science labs, but outside the door he hovers. "I'm sorry, Astrid. I *want* to go with you."

"Do you, Mo? You have a lot of weeks to play music. This

is, like, a once-in-a-lifetime trip. Literally, in my case, since if I ever go back to Sedona after this, I'll be a corpsicle."

"Will you stop saying that?"

"If you're not coming on the road trip, you don't get a say in the terminology."

The second bell sounds, and my chemistry classmates shove past us into the lab. Ms. Sikowitz comes to the doorway.

"Astrid, is my class interrupting your social time?" She says it good-naturedly, though, because Ms. Sikowitz is cool like that.

"Sorry. Coming." I turn back to Mo impatiently, waiting for him to say something that'll make me feel better.

But "Good luck on your test" is the best he can come up with.

29.

AFTER SCHOOL, I DON'T BOTHER TO FIND
Mohit or Chloe, and I muster the energy to get off campus
faster than usual so I can walk home alone. It's one of those
blustery early winter days, blue sky but sharp air, and it feels
surprisingly good to tromp through the cold without company. My thoughts settle as I walk. I'm annoyed at Mo, but it's
not really about the road trip. I want him to come, of course,
and if he can't, I'm not sure my mom will still let Chloe and
me go alone—given that she thinks of Mo as the Responsible
One among the three of us. But really, that's not what it is.

I'm mad because he'd said he wanted in. For all of it. And
now he wants to escape to his music. I kick a pile of crusty
leaves out of my path, and a sharp twinge shoots through my
spine from the exertion. Then I do it again anyway, because
I can.

I know it's not fair to be angry at Mo for wanting to rehearse for the Regattabar. It's easily the biggest gig of his life
so far. Plus, he's right. I did tell him he should join the quartet.

He probably would've given up the chance if I'd asked him to. But I don't want to be *that* person, either.

The TV is on when I get home, which is totally weird. Could Mom have left in such a hurry this morning that she left the news on? She rarely even watches the news anymore, ever since, as she puts it, "our national politics became a shitshow of epic proportion."

I drop my stuff by the door and plod into the living room. Liam's on the couch under a fleece blanket.

"Hey," he says, barely looking up from the television.

"Um, hey?" I sit down next to him and let out a heavy breath. It feels good to be seated again. "Are you home alone?"

"Yup."

"Do you want to tell me why?"

Liam grunts and pauses the program he's watching. "I felt sick, so Mom picked me up after lunch. But then I didn't have a fever and she had to go back to work and no one could come stay with me, so she said I should stay right here and not move until you got home. Except to go to the bathroom. I'm allowed to move to do that." He un-pauses the program.

"Oh. Okay." I watch for a minute with him. It's some cartoon involving Hobbit-like creatures. "Are you feeling better now?"

He ignores me.

I take the remote from him and mute it, prompting a halfhearted protest. "Liam, are you okay?"

This time he shrugs.

"Were you really feeling sick?"

Another shrug.

"You want to tell me what's up?"

"Nothing."

I drape myself over Liam so my eyes are about an inch from his. He ducks one way, but I follow him. Then he shifts the other way, and I follow him again. Finally, he tries to shove me off, but then a smile creeps across his face. "Astrid! You're so annoying."

"It's my job. Now tell me why you came home from school if you're not really sick."

"I *was* sick," he whines. Then he pauses. "Well, I felt sick. I had a headache."

"Uh-huh."

"And a stomachache."

"Well, which was it?"

"Both, I swear!"

"Okay. What are we watching?"

He perks up considerably as he explains the intricacies of a near-future universe populated by goblins and trolls and half-humans. I try to look interested while my brain glazes over.

"Hey, Astrid?"

"Hey, Liam."

"Can you really freeze your body so you can wake up again one day? Is that real?"

I sigh. I wondered when this question was going to come

up. "Look, bud. It's not quite that simple. It's more . . . an experiment."

"Like a science experiment?"

"Kind of, yeah."

"So, like, we could read about you in science class?"

"I mean, not you, probably. But maybe some kids in the future. Maybe."

I can see his brain at work, considering all this. "Do you think you'll be able to wake up, like, for my college graduation?"

My brother. Possibly the only eight-year-old on the planet for whom his future college graduation is already a milestone he's planning for. One million very small daggers poke one million very small holes in my heart.

"Oh, Liam. It's not really like that." I try to put an arm around him, but it's awkward. I can't blame him when he kind of wiggles away. "I'm sorry, bud."

"Kieran's mom says you could probably see my college graduation anyway, from heaven. So at least there's that."

"You talked to Kieran's mom about me?"

He squirms in his seat like he's rapidly tiring of this conversation and wants to return to the near-future of goblins and trolls.

"I mean, it's okay if you did. It's just . . . I don't really believe in heaven, you know? Do you?"

"I don't know." He seems guarded, like he doesn't want to embarrass himself in front of me but this heaven thing maybe doesn't sound so bad, all things considered.

"We don't really know what happens after a person dies," I say. "No one does. So whatever you believe, that's fine. Nothing's impossible."

"Okay," he says, zoning out toward the television. "Do we have to talk about this anymore?"

"Do we have to keep watching this weird program?"

"Dude, it's so good!" He launches into another explanation of what I've been missing. I un-pause the television and smooth out Liam's fleece blanket so it's covering both of us.

I think I'm half asleep when the doorbell rings.

Liam hops up. "Yeah?" he says into the intercom.

"Hey. It's Mohit. Can I come up?"

Liam presses the buzzer without replying and unlocks the front door. A minute later, we hear the elevator doors opening down the hall, and Mo lets himself in.

"In here!" I call toward the front hall. He appears in the entryway to the living room, his cheeks flushed with cold. I don't get up. I figure I'll let him do the talking if he has something to say.

Mohit puts his sax case down by his feet and rubs his hands together to warm them up. "Okay."

That's it. *Okay.* The television keeps blaring between us.

"Okay?" I ask.

"Okay. The MIT guys said we could schedule some extra rehearsals the week before and after our trip."

"*Our* trip?" I try not to give away too much hope in my voice.

"And my parents made me promise to bring my horn and practice along the way. So you'll have to put up with that."

I push myself off the couch. His body is chilly when I scrunch up next to him. "I'll put up with that."

Mohit leans down to kiss me, and Liam fake-chokes. "Gross, guys. Gross."

30.

INSIDE ITS QUIRKY RED EXTERIOR, THE SUN-
dried Tomato is like a tiny, run-down studio apartment that
has gone untouched since maybe the late seventies, based on
my limited knowledge of that era of interior design. Behind
the front seats, there's a vinyl-upholstered bench seat on each
side running parallel under the windows. Both sides are
patched in spots with silver duct tape, a few tufts of white fluff
poking out through the cracks. A small table folds down from
the wall to make a dining nook. There's a sink, a mini-fridge,
and, at the back, a bathroom with an accordion door like you'd
find on a Megabus, with a showerhead over the toilet.

"We won't be using that, will we?" Mohit asks as he surveys the bathroom doubtfully.

"Um, no," I say. "Hence the motel reservations. But this
is pretty sweet for the road."

Against all my expectations, our first two vlog episodes
managed to raise almost enough money to cover our motel

costs, plus gas. Mom gave me a meal budget—"Consider it a per diem" were her exact words.

Chloe bounds up the steps into the Tomato. Her arms are full of canvas shopping bags. "Mom C sent provisions!"

She flips down the folding table and starts unpacking one of the bags: bananas, apples, a jar of organic no-sugar-added peanut butter, veggie sticks, kale chips, single-serving Greek yogurts in an array of fruit combinations, and some Tupperware concoctions I can't identify.

"Veggie lasagna, leftover saag paneer," she adds, as if reading my mind.

"Saag paneer?" Mohit says, raising an eyebrow. "Your mother cooks Indian food?"

Chloe scoffs. "Of course not. It's leftover takeout from last night. We've only done takeout post-separation anyway."

I look at Mo hopefully. "Did *your* mom cook us anything for the road?" Mrs. Parikh is a great cook when she has the time, but she works long hours in some executive-level job having to do with clean energy production.

"She was too busy at work this week. She did give me forty bucks, though." He shrugs. "I guess we can see a movie on Mama Parikh when we get to wherever it is we're stopping first?"

"Margate, New Jersey," Chloe says from the driver's seat. "And we don't need to see a movie. We're visiting Lucy the Elephant."

"What the hell is that?" Mo asks.

Chloe tosses the guidebook at him. "First sticky note."

He opens to the marked page and starts reading. "Lucy the Elephant is six stories high and is listed on the National Park Registry of Historical Landmarks." He wrinkles his nose and looks up. "We're visiting a giant elephant *statue*? This is not even a real elephant."

"Would you want to see a real elephant on a beach on the Jersey Shore? Seems a smidge cruel, doesn't it?" I say.

"Fine, but what is the point of this excursion? Aren't we just wasting time on our way to Arizona?"

"The point, Mr. Good Humor, is that we're going on a road trip," Chloe says. "And road trips are about kitsch!"

"I thought this road trip was about cryopreservation."

"Are you going to ruin this trip with an incessant critical analysis of everything we do, or are you going to let us all enjoy ourselves?"

Chloe grumbles something else under her breath, but I ignore her. I stretch out on one of the bench seats and put my feet on Mo's lap. "I like your incessant critical analysis," I say. "But also Chloe's right. This road trip is about All the Kitsch."

"Fine. You're the boss." Mo sighs. "Feel okay?" He kneads the backs of my calves gently.

I nod. "Just stiff. Per usual."

"Okay, the hotspot is working," Chloe says. "Are we ready for takeoff?" When she turns around, her face is flushed with more energy than I can imagine mustering for anything at this point, and I love her for it.

Mohit squeezes my leg. "I think your fans want to say goodbye one more time."

Outside, Mom and Liam are emerging from our building with yet another bag of stuff. We've already weighed the Tomato down with more pain meds, fluids, hot and cold compresses, and fuzzy slippers than I can count, not to mention my new friend the Oxygen Tank and its constant companion, the Annoying Plastic Cannula.

Liam bounces into the Tomato. "Whoa! This is awesome!"

"Want the tour, dude?" Chloe offers. She shows him the bathroom, even runs the shower for a minute so he can see how it gets the whole "room" wet.

"Cool!"

Mom sits next to me. "You're sure about this?" she asks quietly. I still can't believe she's letting me go.

"We'll be fine, Mom. I promise."

"You'll keep in touch with me constantly, right? Text, phone, Facebook, et cetera?"

"All of the above. Except, can you please get off Facebook? It's not good for your blood pressure."

"Except, *hello*," Chloe interjects. "That's where most of our traffic is coming from. The people, they still love the Facebook."

"See?" Mom says. "The people still love the Facebook. And I am the people."

"Fine, fine."

"And you'll call Dr. Klein's office if anything seems amiss, or you have questions about the pain meds, or anything at all?"

"We're going to be gone for a week."

She pulls me into her chest and buries her face in the top of my head. "I know, I know. I'm just—I can't believe I'm letting you do this on your own. World's Okayest Parenting Award, right here."

"Mom. *Mom.*"

"What, baby?"

"Suffocating. Me."

She releases my head a little bit. "Sorry. You know, when you were a baby I used to genuinely worry that I'd cuddle you so hard I'd squish you." Mom squeezes me all over again. "I just *love-love-love* you so *much-much-much*." She presses my cheeks together between her palms.

"Okay, okay. I hear you. I love you, too. And I think you're in the clear on the parenting behavior on this one. Remember, you're giving me the keys to my destiny. Isn't that what all parents strive for?"

Mom raises an eyebrow. "If that's what we're calling this." Then she looks at Mo. "Mohit, you're in charge. If she's hurting, or if anything seems off at all, I want to know about it. I don't care what she says."

"Roger that."

"Why am I not in charge, Maxine?" Chloe asks from the driver's seat, smirking at us.

"No comment, Chloe, my love."

"And what about me? I get no say in this whatsoever?" I say. "I'm not dead yet, you know."

"You're an unreliable witness." Mom kisses me one more time. "All right, Liam-boy, let's let these guys get on the road.

And I have your list of motels, but if you change any of your plans—which you should if you get tired and you didn't get as far as you expected—I want details *immediately*. Got that? If I spot-check these motels, I expect to find you wherever you said you were going to be."

"*Are* you going to spot-check the motels?"

"I am not ruling it out. So don't make us both regret it."

"Bye, Mommy." I kiss her cheek. "Bye, dude," I say to Liam.

"Bye, baby. Bye, partners-in-crime. Drive very, very safely. Both of you." My mother looks from Chloe to Mohit and back again, her best serious-mom expression plastered all over her face.

"Don't worry, Maxine. I've been driving the Tomato since I got my license."

"Which was all of a year ago, Chloe."

"Details. I'm an expert. And Mohit is . . . fine."

We all look at Mo.

"I've been practicing!" He crosses his arms defiantly.

"Careful," Mom says. "Under the speed limit, always. No texting and driving. No loud music. Constant contact with your mother."

I let out a grand sigh. "Mom, we got it. All of it."

"Fine. I love you."

"Love you, too, Mom."

As we pull away from the curb, Mom and Liam wave frantically until we're almost out of sight. I see Mom wipe her face, then shake it off. My own cheeks get hot, and I swallow back tears. Even though I'm super ready to go on this trip, and even though it's only for a few days, I'll miss them.

"Hey," Mo says quietly. "You okay?"

"Yeah. Are we really going to Arizona to see the corpsicles?"

"Can we please stop calling them that?"

The sun is barely rising as Chloe eases the Tomato onto 93 South. She honks the horn. "Next stop! Points southwest."

And just like that, weighed down with only about a thousand pounds of snacks, a veritable pharmacy, and the feeling that we are driving toward a future none of us can imagine, we're on our way.

31.

WE'RE CHATTY FOR THE FIRST COUPLE OF hours, arguing over the radio (Chloe wants only Top 40; Mohit claims we're rotting our brains with even one round of Justin Bieber) and breaking out the snacks already. By the time the day is fully awake, though, I'm tired and rest my head against the side of the Tomato's bench seat. The old vinyl crunches under my cheek, but I'm too exhausted to get my pillow, or even to ask Mo to get it for me.

"Wake me when we get to New Jersey."

We've decided to make the first day's drive a relatively short one, just far enough to hit Lucy the Elephant in the afternoon and crash for the night. Even so, it suddenly seems like a very long first leg.

When I wake, the Tomato is quiet and still. I sit up gingerly, as I always do now, assessing my body one inch at a time. Head? Not throbbing. Back? Sore from the twisted position

I've been sleeping in, probably, but not terrible. Legs? Sturdy enough beneath me, it seems.

I'm alone. Outside, I see Chloe pumping gas into the Tomato's belly, staring absently out at the long road in front of her. Mo's nowhere to be seen, but I'm guessing he's peeing. Mohit has the smallest bladder of any guy I've ever met.

I stretch and manage to lower myself out of the vehicle without incident. Wherever we are, I can't smell the sea. So I didn't sleep quite all the way to the Jersey Shore, then.

The rest stop is called Benny's 24 Hours, according to half-burned-out neon signage over the front door. Looks like your standard cigarettes/lottery tickets/slushies kind of place—not one of those new fancy rest areas with multiple dining options and arcade games and a playground and dog run off the parking lot. When we used to stop on the way to visit my grandmother in upstate New York every Thanksgiving, Mom always made us choose the healthiest food on offer, which seemed like it defeated the purpose of a road trip. Liam and I would negotiate our way into sharing a milkshake or a small McNuggets or something—anything—to go with our limp, days-old rest-area salads. After Dad left, Mom started packing a cooler full of snacks and sandwiches for our trips to Grandma's, and she'd drive almost straight there, as fast as we could go without getting pulled over. We didn't stop at all, unless someone *really* had to pee.

Mohit emerges from Benny's. His face lights up when he sees me. "You're up!" He kisses me. "Hey, this place is owned by Parikhs! We could probably get a deal on a room if we want."

"A room?"

Mo nods toward a motel behind Benny's. "Same owners, obviously. I told you Gujaratis are the kings of lodging." Gujarat, the state in northwest India where Mohit's parents were born, has apparently produced an outsize proportion of motel owners in America, among other entrepreneurial ventures.

"Where are we?"

"Not in Margate yet, that's for sure. Still in New York."

We've been on the road for what feels like an age already, but *New York*? That's practically around the corner. I feel a twinge in my spine and try to shrug it off. Arizona feels far away.

"I should probably update my mom on our whereabouts."

Mohit holds up a mini apple pie contained in a small paper wrapper. "Pie?"

"Ah, you're a genius." I take a bite. It's microwave-hot and too sweet and really good, the kind of treat Liam and I would've begged for on a road trip.

"I've been texting her every time we cross a state line," he says. "Which, to be fair, has only been twice because, like I said, we're still in New York."

"Thanks," I say through another bite of too-hot pie. "You a ve-y goo boy-feh."

"What was that?"

I fan at my mouth, chewing while trying not to scald myself.

"Uh-huh. I'd like to hear whatever you said just then one more time, without the pie." Mo raises an eyebrow at me.

"Was it something like 'You're a very good boyfriend'? I'm just wagering a guess. Tell me if I'm wrong."

He certainly seems perkier than he did when we set off, and it's a relief. I don't think I could take a whole road trip to and from Arizona with Mo and Chloe bickering with each other. I stick my tongue out at him, revealing a mouthful of pie.

The Tomato honks—or more like squawks—at us from its parking spot, and Chloe leans out the front door. "We're gassed up, and your third wheel would like to get a move on now, thanks!"

Chloe makes Mohit drive for a while, through the rest of southern New York and finally, mercifully, over the border into New Jersey, so she can film another vlog entry and post it to our site.

"So we're on our way to Arizona," I say, unbearably awkwardly I'm sure, into the camera. The light from outside filters through the smudged windows of the Tomato as stretches of flat, identical highway speed by. "We're going to see the, uh, the cryopreservation facility there, which is where I would probably, um, be living—though not technically *living*—if I'm able to preserve my body. So, yeah. That's it."

I stop there. Chloe looks at me dully. "That's it?" she says, pausing the camera. "Can you think of something a smidge more dynamic to tell your fans?"

"Chloe, I have no fans. The people watching these videos are, like, twelve of our classmates and your mothers."

She rolls her eyes. "All of whom are people who gave you the money to take this little road trip, I might add. Not to mention the in-kind donation of the Tomato. So we may as well make them a video they can enjoy."

I sigh. I don't know how to make a video of myself right now that people can "enjoy." We're not on some quirky made-for-reality-television road trip. We're in an RV, true, which is pretty cool, but when said RV is taking you to Arizona to check out the facility where at some point soon your posthumous body might be contained at subzero temperatures while your loved ones falter on in their lives without you, it's not that cute.

I don't say that to Chloe, or in the video, obviously. I get what she's trying to do, which is be helpful. Raise money. Get me what I want for my dying wish. She's a good friend like that. But I'm still having a hard time reconciling the two things—the privacy of illness and death with the public nature of posting videos to the internet and asking strangers for money. It gives me a twisty, sour feeling in my stomach every time I think about it.

But I won't ask my mother for any more money than she's already contributed. She doesn't have more to give, even if I didn't feel guilty about asking for it. So I push the sour-stomach feeling aside and pull my mouth into a smile, for the fans.

32.

WE FINALLY COME OFF THE GARDEN STATE
Parkway and follow the GPS onto Route 563. Shortly there-
after, we find ourselves in Margate, where Lucy the Elephant
looms large—six stories, just like the guidebook promised—
right over the water. In the legions of great kitsch lining
American roadsides, Lucy, it turns out, is pretty epic.

Chloe insisted that we spend our first night in the motel
adjacent to Lucy's park. It's obviously off-season, so it's quiet
when we check in. It's unclear if there are any other guests at
all, actually. The kid at the front desk looks about our age
and bored out of her mind.

"You want to see the elephant?" she says, absently, like
she's possibly high. We indicate that yes, we do indeed want
to see the elephant. (Why else would we be in this motel in
the middle of a Saturday in the dead of winter?) She snaps a
piece of gum and shrugs as she hands us our room keys—one
for me and Chloe, one for Mohit, per all our parents' instructions. "Last tour starts at three thirty."

The rooms are standard-issue coastal-town cheap, the same horrible wallpaper and horrible bedspreads that seem to have been sold in bulk to all the motels across the country. I rest for a minute on one of the double beds in our room while Chloe pees.

"Should you bring your oxygen tank to the elephant?" she calls from the bathroom, kicking the door halfway open so I can hear her.

I look at the tank and cannula, coiled up and waiting for me in the corner. They're in the wheely cart, but it'll be a pain to lug up what I imagine are quite a lot of stairs in Lucy's leg.

"No. I'll be okay."

Chloe flushes. "Are you sure? Mo can carry it. It can't weigh much more than his sax case, and he never goes anywhere without that."

"No. I'm sure. I can climb the elephant on my own."

We're the only people on the last tour of the day. Another kid close enough to our age and apparently not as interested in Lucy as we are leads the tour with a mild air of irritation, like he was hoping the last tour would get canceled, but then we showed up.

The stairs are in Lucy's back left leg, and though it's a spiral staircase, I realize with some relief that there aren't actually *that* many stairs. Chloe bounds up ahead, peppering the poor tour guide with questions based on the two paragraphs of Lucy's history she read in our guidebook.

Mohit follows a step or two behind, spotting me, I can tell. "She looks like an Indian elephant," he muses. "So why is her name Lucy? I've never met an Indian Lucy."

"I have no idea, Mo." I concentrate on walking, one foot in front of the other, one step, then another. I pause midway to catch my breath. A few minutes later, we come up into Lucy's belly, where Chloe is already watching a video about the statue's history.

You wouldn't know it from the outside, but it's quite spectacular in the belly of an elephant. I count twenty-two windows in every direction. The tour guide musters some enthusiasm when he tells us to look out Lucy's huge glass eyes, which give us a perfect view of the ocean and the beach below. The beach is empty, and for a moment it feels like we're the only people in the world, our little group of weirdos on a weird field trip. No cancer, no frozen bodies ahead of us, just me, Mo, and Chloe. Well, and the tour guide.

"Hey, look," Mo says. "She has a pane in the butt. Get it?" He's cracking up, pointing to the window in Lucy's rear.

"I see what you did there."

The late-afternoon winter sun shimmers through Lucy's windows. Up another set of stairs, the guide leads us into the howdah, the carriage perched on Lucy's back, for an even better view of the ocean as far as we can see.

"Whoa," Chloe says, under her breath. "This is good."

"Right?" I grin at her.

Mo wraps an arm around me, and I think of the first time we took in a beautiful view together, our first conversation about God, the beginnings of becoming each other's favorite people.

It's cold up there, even in the sun, with the wind blowing pretty hard off the water. I savor a long, deep inhale of salt air. From here, the rest of the trip will be inland. Who knows when—if—I'll smell the ocean again.

Later, after we've eaten cheeseburgers, the kind that are pressed perfectly thin against the grill, at a divey beachside restaurant, I call Mom.

"How is it?" she asks.

"Pretty great so far. We climbed a giant elephant and saw the ocean."

Mom laughs, and for a moment she sounds like her old self, the person she was before I got sick and my sickness started to define how much fun she was allowed to have, how hard she was allowed to laugh. Her laughing got rationed. At least, it seems that way to me.

Anyway, she laughs. "That does sound perfect, my love."

"It was."

I'm so exhausted from this long day basically sitting in a moving vehicle that it's all I can do to peel my clothes off and collapse into bed. Steam from Chloe's shower filters into the room and makes me feel a little sticky; there must not be a vent in the bathroom. I hear her singing to herself, an Aretha Franklin song we heard on the radio earlier.

You better think—think! Think about what you're trying to do to me!

I smile, picturing Chloe grooving under the hot water, maybe holding a travel-size shampoo bottle as a mic. She's in a good mood. I'm glad. Maybe she's gotten lost in the moment of all of this and let herself forget—or just push aside—the real reason we're on this trip in the first place. I wish I could do the same thing.

I reach for my phone, but the battery's dead, and instantly I know the charger is still sitting in the Tomato. Go figure. There's no way I'm getting out of this bed and taking myself out to the parking lot to retrieve it. Instead, I grab the video camera off Chloe's bed, prop it up on my chest on top of the covers, and start talking.

33.

Things I'll miss when I'm dead (a partial list, continued):
The smell of the ocean
Thin cheeseburgers with pickles and onions
People who know me as well as I know myself
Kitsch
Beautiful views

34.

ON OUR WAY TOWARD THE MIDDLE OF THE
country, we spend hours on very straight roads that cut clean
paths through snow-covered meadows in Pennsylvania, and
pass the occasional horse-drawn buggy in Amish country. We
briefly cross West Virginia, then enter Ohio. As the country
speeds by outside, we see almost nothing of note on either side
of the highway, just the occasional motel with a covered in-
ground pool out front and a blinking neon sign advertising
air-conditioning, cable, vacancies. It's not flashy country, but
it's beautiful in its own way.

At the end of the twelve-hour driving day, we stop at a
diner somewhere in Indiana. It's a twenty-four-hour kind of
place frequented by truckers. The parking lot is mostly empty
except for a couple of eighteen-wheelers, which I suspect are
driven by the handful of guys sitting solo at the long counter.
We take a corner booth, since we have our pick.

"So, get excited," Chloe says after we've ordered. "Big
day tomorrow."

"Dare I ask?" Mo says.

"We are going to the geographic center of the contiguous United States. Think of the photo opportunities!"

"How far out of our way are we going to hit these interim destinations?" Mo asks. "I mean, not that I really want to know."

"Look, we'd be going farther out of our way if we were going to the geographic center of the United States *including* Alaska and Hawaii, because that's somewhere in South Dakota. This is barely a detour. Anyway, you knew what you were signing up for here."

The waitress brings our food. I slept through a lot of the ride today, but I still feel tired. Bone tired, the kind of tired sleep doesn't relieve. I push my soup around in the bowl and watch the occasional hunk of chicken float to the surface, then disappear again.

"You okay?" Chloe asks. She's usually not the concerned one.

"Yeah. Just tired." I muster a smile. "Geographic center of the contiguous United States! Woo!"

Chloe frowns. "We can skip it and keep driving," she offers. "It's not a big deal."

But it is a big deal. This is my trip, my closest-thing-I'll-ever-get-to-a-college-spring-break-road-trip road trip. I'm not missing it because I have a brain tumor.

"No way, we're not skipping it." I gulp down some soup, which is straight-from-the-microwave scorching hot. "I want to see the geographic center of the contiguous United States, dammit!"

Chloe exchanges a look with Mohit, who shrugs.

"Okay, if you're sure," she says. "It's going to be really cool, because I was *thinking* . . ."

I tune out as Chloe babbles on about the vlog episode she wants to film once we get there. Under the table, Mohit tickles my knee. I put my hand over his and trace the fingers I know so well. In my mind, I can see the clipped nails in their deep beds, the tiny patches of dark hair on his knuckles, the hardened bump on his left ring finger because of the weird way he holds a pencil.

I miss him already, too.

We check in to the aptly named Plain View Motel, two nondescript stories just off the interstate with nothing to see from any of its windows, even if it weren't pitch-black outside. As I climb into bed, I hear the muted sounds of Mo's saxophone coming from the room next door. I press my cheek to the wall. He's playing something I don't recognize, a new piece, probably. I can imagine him playing it at the Regattabar in a couple of months, the lights shining on him in the otherwise darkened club.

"Mo," I whisper. Then I repeat it a little louder, almost at normal volume. "Mo."

I know he can't hear me. The walls are thin but not that thin, and whenever he's playing I have to yell to be heard over his sax anyway, especially when he's in the world of his music.

"Mo," I say again. Of course, still no response. He keeps playing. "I don't know if I want to do this anymore."

"Are you talking to me?" Chloe calls from the bathroom, her mouth full of toothpaste.

"I didn't say anything."

It's a confession I'm not ready to be held accountable for. Not yet.

Things I'll miss when I'm dead (a partial list, continued):
High school and college and med school graduations
Making a major discovery in neuroscience research and
    having it published in a journal
Fixing people through science
Science, in general

36.

THE GEOGRAPHIC CENTER OF THE CONTIGU-
ous United States, turns out, is in Lebanon, Kansas, and it's
marked by a faded blue plaque on a monument near the side of
the road. It's just a pile of rocks, really, a little stack of stones
on a frozen, snow-encrusted patch of grass. Nearby, there's a
small white building with a simple cross on the roof, labeled
U.S. CENTER CHAPEL. It's like the tiny house of churches, a
chapel made for Stuart Little.

"Guys, we can stop off for a quick prayer after Chloe's
done filming," I say. "Do you think this is, like, hallowed
ground or something? Did you read about this, Clo? If I leave
a drop of my blood on the altar at the geographic center of the
contiguous United States, will I be magically cured?"

"Worth a shot," Chloe says absently as she sets up her
camera.

"Power of prayer, right?"

"Oh, stop," Mo says. He leans against the Tomato, arms

crossed over his chest and a wool hat pulled low over his ears. "You can be an atheist and still not be a jerk."

"Sorry." I blow on my hands. It's hard to believe we'll be in Arizona after just one more day of driving, where the weather app on my phone tells me it'll be in the eighties.

"Also," Mohit adds, "you're the one for whom we are driving across the country to visit a *cryopreservation* facility, I might remind you. Hardly a matter of scientific certainty."

"Fine, fine, you win."

"Okay." Chloe points the camera in my general direction while I hop up and down from one foot to the other. "Action."

"Hi, everyone. Uh, so, we are here in Lebanon, Kansas, which is the geographic center of the contiguous United States. Sorry, Alaska and Hawaii."

"What are we doing here?" Chloe asks from behind the camera.

I laugh. "I mean, who *wouldn't* want to come to the geographic center of the contiguous United States? Are you jealous, yet?" I'm getting more used to talking to this invisible audience, the mystery people on the other side of these videos who will think they know me based on whatever it is I say on camera.

"We're seeing the country," I add. "Not quite coast to coast, but coast to corpsicles, one might say."

I stop to think for a moment. We're on our way to visit the corpsicles, of course. We're seeing All the Kitsch. But there's also something else I haven't quite articulated to my "fans." Or to myself, for that matter.

"I guess you could also say that I'm taking control of my life for a minute," I say. "When you're sick, you don't get to choose much. I mean, most people don't get to choose much in this life, period. But, like, when you're sick, everything seems to become just an unfolding of events."

On the other side of the camera, Chloe is still and silent. I see Mohit look up from the guidebook, paying attention all of a sudden. I try to ignore their reactions and press on.

"You're not driving your life—your illness is driving it. So we're on this trip because, I don't know, I wanted to drive my life for a minute. Or in this case, have Chloe and Mohit drive, literally. But I'm doing the figurative driving. You know what I mean."

I stop there. No one says anything.

"Can you hear me okay?"

When Chloe puts down the camera, her face looks all funny, sad and twisty in a way Chloe never looks. "Yeah. We heard you," she says. "Let's go. It's cold out here."

37.

AS PREDICTED, THE COUNTRY GETS WARMER
and warmer as we move southwest. By the time we cross
into Arizona, it's seventy-five degrees out, and we stop by the
side of the road to film me straddling the state line and to
stretch our limbs in the sun. I can practically feel the vitamin
D seeping into my skin.

My father's commune isn't far from the Petrified Forest
National Park in northeastern Arizona. I was here before, with
Dad and Liam, a few years ago. Dad took us hiking through the
park, showed us the fossils the area is known for, especially
fallen trees that were apparently alive during the Late Triassic
Period, which is like a bajillion years ago (roughly 225 million,
in fact). Liam thought it was absurdly cool. I was thirteen,
Dad had been living out here for a year or so, and I was mad
about the whole situation, so I didn't want to *act* impressed—
but I was impressed, too.

"You all right?" Mo asks as we roll through Apache County.
The land is flat and arid, with a huge, nearly cloudless sky.

I nod vaguely. It's been over a year since I saw my father, and I'm not sure what I'll say when we get there, since the last time I talked to him he indicated that I'd pretty much brought my cancer on myself. I guess I'll figure it out when we get there.

The Ranch itself looks like the kind of summer camp I never went to because I dislike woods and tents and things buzzing around my head. We pass through a tall wooden gate—which Mo has to get out and open, then close behind us, per the instructions on the sign hanging from it—and then follow the length of driveway that winds through a wide, open field. At the end of the driveway, there's the main lodge, where Dad takes his phone calls and where the group shares their meals and whatever else they do. As we pull up, I note new solar panels on the lodge roof.

Beyond the lodge, narrow and mostly unpaved roads curve around the land, with turnoffs at a series of tiny houses. Each comes with its own patch of scrappy lawn out front and what look like various accoutrements for capturing water. Less summer camp, more retirement community for the kind of people who aren't registered to vote but complain a lot about the government, I guess.

There are no house numbers, but each structure has a name. Dad's is called "Bliss'd Out." I'm not sure which drives me more nuts, the use of the outdated slang or the dropped "e." The house is white, like all the other houses, with green shutters and windowboxes filled with tiny purple flowers and a range of herbs. There's a garden and a well, and two bicycles lean against the side of the house, each with a wicker basket and a bell.

My father steps outside just as we pull up to the front door. He plasters a grin over his face, blocks his eyes from the late-afternoon sun with a callused hand. His skin is more wrinkled than I remember it, more tanned, and he looks like he hasn't shaved in a while.

"You made it!"

I climb out of the Tomato. "Hi, Dad."

"We'll be back in an hour?" Mohit asks, leaning out the Tomato's open door. "Unless you want us here?"

I shake my head. "That's all right. Go find a Friendly's or something. This won't take that long."

"We're in Arizona, Astrid," Chloe says. "No Friendly's."

"Really?"

"Really."

"All right, well, Chili's, then. McDonald's. Any establishment that sells french fries."

Dad waves and approaches the vehicle. "Mo-heat, hi there!"

"It's Mohit," I say under my breath.

"What's that?"

"Nothing, Dad."

"Hi, Mr. Ayeroff. Good to see you again," Mo says. Then he closes the Tomato's door, and Chloe wrestles a three-point turn and maneuvers them back along the narrow path. I watch its dusty red rear waddle around the corner, and then they're gone.

"They didn't want to come in? They could've joined us." Dad ushers me into the tiny house, where he's got a tiny fire burning in the tiny woodstove, even though it's hot as hell.

"It's okay. They'll go get lunch or something."

"Mo-heat couldn't take the heat, huh? Didn't want to have a one-on-one with your old man?"

I ignore him, and survey the empty room. There's a miniature kitchen that takes up one wall, with a wooden ladder climbing up to a loft bed overhead, a bathroom with a composting toilet. The decor is what I can only describe as generically spiritual: a small bronze Buddha in one corner, textiles that look like the kind of faux–Native American prints sold at Urban Outfitters, a framed scroll with Chinese lettering that probably means something completely nonsensical.

"Where's Suzanne?"

"She'll be here. She's at the acupuncturist. How about a walk?"

I don't really want to go for a walk—my whole body hurts, and a headache creeps in behind my eyes—but I don't feel like spelling out my various ailments for my father, so I shrug noncommittally and let him take it as a yes.

We set off on a narrow footpath along the edge of an expanse of land they call the Sweetmeadow. Dad walks faster than I can keep up with, but the path is only wide enough to walk single file anyway, so it doesn't matter.

"It's good to see you, my girl. I've missed you, you know," he says as he tromps ahead of me, talking to the air.

"Have you?" I can't get out much more than a couple of

words at a time, with all my energy focused just on putting one foot in front of the other.

"It's not easy to get to Boston. It's a long haul, and we don't own a car, so. You know how it is."

"Yeah. I know. Long bike ride, I guess." I stop and put my hands to my knees, bending over to steady myself. The earth sways a little bit beneath me, and bright dots cloud my vision.

Dad stops and turns. When I straighten up, Dad's furrowing his tanned brow at me, concerned. "You seem weaker than the last time I saw you. You all right?"

The dots, little satellites made by my tumor of stars, scatter slowly to the edges of my sight lines and then dissipate. "Besides the recurrence of my brain tumor? Sure. Peachy."

My father blinks several times. His hair has gotten longer, and he's got it tucked back in a man bun that seems particularly sad—sadder even than a normal man bun, and those are sad enough—because it's gone fully gray. The lenses in his glasses are thicker than I remember, and he's gained weight; even living here, "off the earth," he's grown a gut that pokes at his moth-eaten sweater.

"I love you, Astrid. I'm sorry this is happening to you."

I swallow. There's nothing to say. Dad takes his glasses off and wipes a hand over his eyes, though they look dry.

"And this . . . cryopreservation facility you're visiting. You think this has real potential?"

I haven't talked to him about our final destination, so Mom must have filled him in.

"I don't know, Dad. It's a long shot. It's just something I'm curious about."

"Well, I guess that makes sense. You always did love your science."

It gives me a pang of longing in my gut, the way he says it, a reminder that he is in fact my father and was part of my everyday life for my first twelve years. He did know me, even if it doesn't feel like that anymore.

"Remember that science fair project where we built the roller coaster?" he says. "That was a good one."

Sixth grade, just when things were starting to go off the rails for my parents but before he left. He must've already been feeling guilty about what he knew he was going to do, because he spent an inordinate amount of time working with me on an elaborate loop-the-loop roller coaster, complete with little cardboard people strapped into the car.

"I did not think that was going to work," I say.

"Nor did I, my girl. Nor did I. We made a good team, though. Anyway, Astrid." He takes a step closer to me on the path and touches my arm. "I'm just sorry that I couldn't—you know, I couldn't do anything about your illness myself. To stop this from happening to you. I mean, your mother—"

Just like that, resentment creeps back in, ruining the moments before. "Come on, Dad. Don't 'your mother' this again, please. You should know better."

"I'm not blaming her. I just wish she had been more open to this lifestyle. To letting go of attachments, and toxins. I think it would've helped her in her own life, too. And I'm not sure you would've ended up like this. That's all I'm saying."

I've heard it before. "I know, Dad. I get it. You think Mom and I manufactured a cancer by living with electricity and indoor plumbing. I've heard."

"That's not what I mean."

"Dad, I'm exhausted. I've had a headache for months now. I don't feel like arguing about what happened to make me sick, or what you can or cannot do about it. Let's just go."

He doesn't say anything. Then he nods back toward the way we've come.

I don't expect to see Suzanne when I push the door open, but suddenly she's right there, filling almost the entire room. She's in the middle of changing her shirt, her bare back facing me.

"Oh god, sorry!" I back up out the door, but she just laughs. Her laugh is like a small child's, the peals of a tiny bell. A moment later, she appears in the doorway, clothed now (barely), with a thin, almost translucent white tank top stretched over what I can now see is a hugely pregnant belly.

I do a double take.

Suzanne smiles at my reaction. "I guess your father didn't tell you?"

Dad clears his throat awkwardly. "We, uh. We hadn't quite gotten there yet."

"We were so excited to tell you in person! You're going

to have a brother. Well, or a sister. I think it's a boy, but we won't know until the birth, of course."

I look at Dad. He didn't seem that excited to tell me, to be honest. If he had been, he might've mentioned it. Now his blue eyes shift from Suzanne to me and back.

"I have a brother," I say.

"Of course," Suzanne says. "I meant, you know, another brother."

"Let's make some tea," Dad says.

I want to run toward the road and try to flag down Mo and Chloe in the Tomato, but my legs won't carry me that far. Instead, I resign myself to waiting until they come back. Dad and Suzanne offer me a "seat" in their "living room," which is basically just one corner with a bunch of pillows strewn over the floor. I lower myself onto one of them, even though it sends a shooting pain up my spine.

She's due right now. More than right now. Hence the acupuncture, she tells me earnestly, running a hand over her stomach.

"Your mother is a midwife now, isn't she?" Suzanne asks brightly.

"Maxine's been a midwife for years, Suze. You know that." Dad sets two mugs of tea in front of us. I take mine and watch a few stray herbs float in the steaming water. Suzanne shoots him an irritated look, as though he's blown her cover. Of course she knows; she's just making small talk, perfectly normal, with her perfectly normal stepdaughter.

"Well, I have so much respect for midwives. I mean, the work they do! They're goddesses, I mean *seriously*. You know, the midwives here will deliver babies who in regular hospitals would just be immediate cesareans. They'll deliver breech babies, eleven pounders—I mean, they're really wonderful. Childbirth has become so medicalized, you know. Giving birth isn't a trauma. Or it doesn't have to be, anyway. But you know that from your mother, I'm sure."

She smiles at me. I don't think she's even thirty. Her skin is peachy and smooth and completely bare of makeup in a way that feels calculated more than accidental, as if she's cultivated a look of not caring what she looks like, when in fact she knows she looks like perfection.

"My mother is a medical professional, not a goddess," I say. "And she's smart enough to know the difference."

I push myself off the absurdly uncomfortable floor cushion—barely making it to vertical—and pull my phone out to call Mo as I make a beeline for the door.

Dad's right behind me. "Astrid." His face is flushed with irritation when he steps outside. "That wasn't necessary."

"You could've told me."

"Told you—"

"About your replacement plan. One kid dies, add a fresh one."

"You know that's not what's happening."

"That's exactly what's happening, isn't it? Or was Suzanne herself the replacement? She's almost young enough."

Dad laughs and shakes his head. A few strands of his man bun come loose. "Keep your voice down if you're going to pitch a fit, Astrid."

"What difference does it make? Do the neighbors not know? You haven't told them about how your first kid is on her way out? Why not? Too embarrassed that we let the toxins of normal life get to us?"

"You're my firstborn, Astrid. You always will be. No one and nothing could ever replace you. Your mother and I grew apart, and I have a different life now. It doesn't mean I don't love you and your brother still."

My eyes sting with warm tears. "My cancer isn't my fault. Or Mom's."

Dad lets out a long breath, and his face softens. "I know that, Astrid. That's not what I meant by what I've said. I'm just worried about you, and I—"

"Well, don't worry anymore. Just get over it. Lucky for you, once I'm gone, you'll net the same number of offspring."

The Tomato comes around the corner, crunching dirt and leaves under its wheels. Mo's driving now, with Chloe in the front seat. When they pull to a stop, I see them both hesitate, wondering if they should get out or stay put.

"Bye, Dad. I'm sure Mom will call you to tell you when I'm dead."

38.

MY HEAD ACHES WORSE THAN BEFORE, A
low pulse behind my eyes that wraps around the back of my
skull, which might be the influence of my brain tumor or my
father, I can't tell. I don't want Mohit and Chloe to worry and
certainly don't want them to give my mother an update that
I'm not doing well. So I tell them I need a nap.

I don't know how long I'm out, but the sound of my own
voice wakes me up. Which is a strange sensation, I might add,
hearing your own voice as though you're dreaming but then it
turns out you're not.

When my eyes adjust to the light in the Tomato, a black
floater, a new one, enters my vision on the left side. I register
that things hurt. And I see that the source of my voice is
Chloe's phone; she's watching vlog footage on the seat across
from me. I catch pieces of what I'm saying over the rumble of
the engine and the road noise outside.

"More things I'll miss . . . thin cheeseburgers . . ."

Chloe notices me waking up. "Hey! Why didn't you tell

me you were filming these little snippets? People are going to love these—they're so personal."

I lunge toward her and grab the phone. "You didn't . . . ?" But yes, there it is. The footage I filmed alone, in private moments, now open for public viewing on our vlog channel.

"This wasn't meant for the vlog, Chloe!"

"What do you mean? You put it on camera, I just assumed that's what it was for."

I'd meant to email the videos to myself and then delete them from the camera, of course, but I couldn't figure out how to do it, and then I forgot. It's my own fault, but the violation stings. "Please take it down."

"Why?"

"Because it's private." Frustrated, lazy tears well up in my eyes.

"What's the matter?" Mohit asks from the driver's seat, his eyes flicking toward us in the mirror.

"I want it *down. Now.*"

"Okay, okay, hold on a second." Chloe takes the phone back from me. "I need to do it on my laptop."

"Do it on your laptop, then."

My heart is racing and I'm not even sure why. I've already opened myself for public consumption with these vlog episodes, haven't I? I've already fed complete strangers on the internet a diet of dying teenager and her quirky hopes for the future. What is so private about these little musings on things I'm afraid to lose?

I don't know. But it feels like one of those dreams where

you find yourself naked in math class. I feel exposed and mortified, like I can't cover myself quickly enough.

"Hey, friend." Chloe puts a hand on my knee. "I'm sorry I posted these. I thought that's what they were for."

I shake my head. "I shouldn't have used the camera. I've been keeping this list on my phone, and then one night the battery was dead and I just . . . I didn't think. It wasn't meant to be part of the vlog. It was just for me. To keep track."

"But look," she says tentatively. "These little clips are already getting more views than the longer episodes. More views means more donations, right? Which means getting closer to your goal. I'm just saying."

I know that the internet is not a place where you can both ask for help and maintain some semblance of privacy. But the idea of more and more strangers watching me—real strangers, not just kids at school, and not just watching but thinking they *know* me—makes my skin buzz with nerves.

"You can take them down if you're uncomfortable, babe," Mohit says from the driver's side. "It's not permanent."

"Okay," Chloe says. "I can take them down, but you know everything on the internet is permanent to some extent. And, Astrid, people are on your side. They're giving you support. And money. They're saying they hope you find what you're looking for, stuff like that. Trust me. This is a good thing."

What I'm looking for. I press my head against the cool of the Tomato's window and let my vision blur as the road speeds by. Outside, the road cuts straight through the red earth. The landscape is dotted with shrubbery and shadowed by mountains in the distance. The sun is starting to set, and the sky is a watercolor of deep orange and purple, colors that hardly seem possible.

When I close my eyes against the light, I can see Older Mohit playing the saxophone, his longish hair now flecked with a few strands of silver. I see myself tapping my foot against a table leg. There's an expensive cocktail in front of me. (Would it be a martini? I don't even know.) Mo opens his eyes briefly—he always plays with them closed when he's not reading music—and smiles across the room, smiling only with his eyes; they crinkle in the corners, just for me.

Will I find what I'm looking for on the other end of this road trip? Or anywhere? It's getting harder and harder to know.

"Let me see the comments," I say, reaching for Chloe's phone.

She snatches it out of my reach. "Oh," she says. "You shouldn't read the comments. On anything. Have you seen people on the internet these days?"

"I thought you said they were supportive."

"Well, yeah, but there's always someone—"

I grab the phone from her anyway and refresh the page. It's my vlog "channel," the one she set up for me with our collection of videos. My intro video, the one we filmed in my bedroom when this road trip was just a crazy idea, is pinned at the top. The others are in a neat row underneath, each accompanied by a thumbnail of my absurd-looking "vlog face"—the one where I look like a super-awkward, exhausted cancer patient with blue hair, trying to be a cool model. I cringe and scroll quickly past the images of myself.

The first few comments are perfectly friendly, if grammatically questionable. Some are from people whose names I recognize.

Astrid we'll miss you but we are pulling for you. Love from your junior class council.

XOXO

Go Astrid go!

And gradually strangers start weighing in.

Good luck in ur journey! Hope science comes thru for u.

Everyone deserves a chance to make a wish and hope for the best. This girl is no different. I hope she finds peace with her decision.

Bravo for you, thank you for sharing your story. I hope you raise money to freeze yourself!!

God is great. May He bless her and keep her safe in this life and the next.

God rest her soul.

Okay, I'm not dead yet. Geez.

My heart starts racing as I scroll farther down, through these strangers' condolences and best wishes and prayers and blessings and all the rest. I've looked at countless comment threads on the internet—I mean, who hasn't—but the experience of reading comments that are meant for me personally is completely, entirely different. The ones that express pity make my stomach turn sour, like I'm somehow duping the commenters into feeling bad for me when they shouldn't really (though I guess they should, to be fair, since the whole death-by-brain-tumor-at-sixteen thing isn't great). The religious ones make me want to roll my eyes—God has done very little good in this situation so far, let's be honest— except I know Mohit would tell me I'm being judgy and I should just accept people's different ways of offering support.

And then there are the ones Chloe and Mo probably don't want me reading.

Give me money please so I don't have to die? Aww poor baby LOL.

Another example of dumbass rich people thinking they can get whatever they want. Why don't her rich parents just pay for it LOL.

God doesn't make mistakes. Obviously this girl is dying for a reason.

Dumb b*@$# deserves whatever she gets.

Poor thing! 2 young 2 die. Stop criticizing when u
don't know what ur talking about. Let her be.

I stop there and look up. Chloe's face is resting against
the back of the passenger seat, watching me.

I feel my cheeks burn. "It's what I thought," I say, handing
the phone back to her. "It's just internet comments."

"I told you not to read them. Look, there's always some
jerk who wants to use an anonymous comment feed to get out
his aggression." She takes the phone from me. "You okay?"

"I'm fine." I lie back down and stare at the silver of the
Tomato's domed ceiling, trying to steady my breath. "I'm not
nuts, though, am I? To even consider this?"

"Astrid," Mo says. "You can't listen to strangers on the
internet."

"I'm not asking strangers on the internet. I'm asking the
two of you. Am I being completely absurd? Do you secretly
think this is an unbelievably terrible, idiotic idea, and you're
just going along with me because I'm dying and you love me
and you feel sorry for me?"

Neither of them responds for a moment.

"I don't feel sorry for you," Mohit says, finally breaking
the silence in the Tomato. "I feel sorry for *me*. And Chloe.
We're the ones left behind. So I think I speak for both of us
when I say we'll do whatever it takes for the possibility of not

losing you forever. If that makes me the absurd one . . . oh well. I guess I am."

I swallow back a rush of tears. "Fine. You can leave the videos up."

No one says anything else; we just drive on to our final motel, a squat white block from the 1970s. A perfectly still, blue kidney-shaped pool, ringed with white lounge chairs, beckons us from the parking lot. As usual, the motel boasts AC, cable, and bad wallpaper. Only this time, with four days of highway and kitsch between us and Boston, we're five minutes down the road from my possible future home.

39.

FROM THE OUTSIDE, THE AMERICAN INSTITUTE for Cryonics Research looks just like the pictures online: a pile of concrete with not a lot of windows. The only thing marking it as different from the usual office park is that it's fenced on all sides and has what appears to be an impressive security system guarding the front entrance.

It's also smack in the middle of the most beautiful place I've ever seen. Sedona is a huge expanse of red desert, lined with steep canyons, tall rock formations, and pine trees (news to me in a desert, but what do I know?). As we pull up, I crack a window and breathe in dry, crystal-clear air.

Mohit maneuvers the Tomato toward the security gate and rolls down the driver's-side window. A woman in an olive-green uniform looks up from her cell phone.

"Can I help you?"

"We're here to see . . . What's his name, Astrid?"

I lean over from the passenger seat. "Dr. Fitzspelt. He's expecting us."

"Name?"

"Astrid Ayeroff."

The woman picks up a landline phone. I can't hear what she says, but as she hangs up, the electronic gate in front of us peels apart. "Straight ahead, parking's on the left."

Now that we're here, I feel like I've been half expecting that this place didn't even exist, that we'd pull up and there'd be a sign in an empty parking lot: HA-HA, SUCKERS! Or nothing at all.

But it's a real place, just a building where science happens. And I'm here to—maybe, somehow—be part of it. There are so many things I'll miss out on, and even if I go ahead with becoming a corpsicle, I'll still probably miss out on all those things because, let's be honest, the likelihood of me waking up and walking out of that freezer one day is, I mean, not good.

But at least I won't miss out on being part of science.

It sends a shiver up and down my spine, just thinking about it.

In real life, Dr. Fitzspelt is a wiry little man with crazy eyebrows, almost bald but with a ring of white hair around the back of his head. I'd been picturing a Dumbledore-type character, but he's more like a scientifically inclined Smeagol, before he turns into Gollum. He's waiting for us in the lobby when we come in. I lean on Mohit for support as I walk, trying to make my limp less obvious to everyone, including myself.

"Astrid Ayeroff! Wonderful to finally meet you in the flesh, my dear." He shakes my hand and then, as introductions go around, Mohit's and Chloe's.

"Thanks for having us."

"Delighted! Delighted! Right this way. I'll give you a tour of the facility, and then we have plenty of time for you to ask questions."

Inside the building, it still feels disappointingly *normal*: a waiting area with a few pieces of drab leather furniture, a coffee table with a pile of outdated magazines, a water cooler. It could be a walk-in health clinic, the first floor of the kind of law firm that advertises on the subway, you name it. The only sign of anything sleek and modern in the slightest is a flat-screen television on one wall playing a video of a family of four prancing to upbeat, tinny music through a field of yellow flowers. I see nothing about death, dying, or freezing your body, but the children are very blond and the couple looks happy in an aggressively heteronormative kind of way, and I think we're supposed to get the message that you, too, could choose *this life*—a life without loss, where the things you have now that you love so much could be waiting for you on the other side of what you've always believed would be the end of everything.

As we follow him, Dr. Fitzspelt is muttering something about new advances even since the symposium. At the elevator, he hits the down button and turns to us, finally quiet. When he smiles, his lips stick together ever so slightly at the edges, and a fine thread of spit keeps them connected when he opens his mouth again to talk.

"Any questions straightaway?" he asks.

I watch the thread of spit, waiting for it to break. It doesn't. I shake my head. So many questions, actually, but none I'm ready to ask.

The elevator takes us down what must be at least three levels underground. On the way, I have a suddenly very urgent feeling like we're trapped in Willie Wonka's chocolate factory, riding the glass elevator in the wrong direction. There's something Wonka-ish about Fitzspelt, too, now that I'm thinking of it: the spark in his eyes as he prepares to show off his life's work, the eagerness to draw us all into his world. It's contagious, a little bit. And at the same time, chilling.

When we step off the elevator, we're met with undecorated concrete corridors and jarring artificial light. Dr. Fitzspelt leads us through a rambling hallway so circuitous it occurs to me that we should be leaving bread crumbs along it if we ever want to find our way back.

Mo slips his hand into mine and catches my eye, asking silently if I'm ready for this, if I'm okay, if I want to turn around and run. The answer to all of those, impossibly, is yes.

"As you know, we have two different options for cryopreservation: whole-body and neuro only. Those obviously have different space requirements, so we do maintain separate rooms here."

"And the difference, again?" Mohit asks.

"Just what it sounds like. Whole-body preservation is our standard package, and our recommended option, but we do offer neurocryopreservation—that's the freezing of just the head, of course—at a lower price point, for those who want it."

Dr. Fitzspelt sounds awfully chipper, more like he's selling levels of cable service than different options for keeping your dead loved one in a freezer for the foreseeable future.

"We can talk more about the difference between those options once you've had a chance to see the facilities. We'll start here."

He pauses in front of what looks like the door to a safe, thick and secured with multiple bolts. He enters a code in the lockbox, and I hear the bolts click open. I squeeze Mohit's hand. Right behind me, I feel Chloe's breath on my neck, anticipating whatever it is we're about to witness.

Inside the cold room are large white cylinders branded with the institute's logo and arranged in three rows. Each cylinder is labeled with an alphanumeric code. The room itself looks like it could be a modern walk-in freezer for a restaurant, or anything, really. There's nothing that says "Frozen bodies here!" No photos of the patients while they were living, no flowers or notes left in front of the freezers. I don't know what I was picturing, exactly, but whatever it was, it wasn't quite this. There's nothing particularly pleasant about it; it's not like the institute is making an effort to offer their preserved patients a nice stay while they're here. But it's not scary or grotesque, either. Mostly, it just looks like what it is: a scientific facility. A lab. A place where a grand experiment is taking place, quietly, out of view.

I exhale with relief, letting go of tension I didn't even realize I was holding in, and drop Mohit's hand.

"These are the whole-body freezers?" I ask.

"Correct. These are what we call whole-body cryopreservation capsules. However, Astrid—and I'll explain more about this later—I encourage you not to think of these simply as 'freezers.' The process of cryopreservation is quite different from that. We're not in a Stephen King novel here. We're scientists." He gives me a gentle, sticky-lipped smile.

"And the families of patients—do they ever come visit?"

Dr. Fitzspelt chuckles, then catches himself, perhaps remembering suddenly that he's talking to a sixteen-year-old who might well be residing here in a few months.

He sighs. "We've had families tour the facilities, like you're doing now. But to be honest—and I'm sorry this sounds so harsh—living loved ones know that our clients are dead. The families, for the most part, view them as gone and proceed with their lives accordingly. To my knowledge, most of our clients have had funerals. Many have grave sites. Occasionally, I do hear from relatives who want to check in on the progress of the science. Mostly, though, I believe people view our facility as . . ."

He pauses, searching for the right words, which is almost surprising considering that he must have this conversation with prospective customers regularly. Or maybe he doesn't.

"I believe people view our facility as another way of putting their loved ones to rest. Just, rather than undergoing the absolute finality of a burial, the person is kept here, with the possibility for revival one day."

Next to me, Mohit sighs a little too loudly. I give him a quick shut-it-down look, but I don't think Dr. Fitzspelt notices.

I cast one last glance around the freezer room. "And what's the process like for, like, what happens? After I . . . die?"

Dr. Fitzspelt gives a quick nod. "Let me show you."

He leads us down the hall to a room that could pass for the set of a *CSI* spinoff—sterile fixtures, gray cabinets lining the walls, a stainless-steel examination table in the center. There's a frame of sorts in one corner, six or seven feet long, with a deep canvas basket stretched across it. Lying in the basket, there's a body.

Okay, it's not a real body. It's a dummy, with a blue plastic pump affixed to its chest, connecting it via thick tubes to a machine with different-colored knobs.

The demo body, I gather.

"As you know, for cryogenic preservation to work, the body must be preserved at the moment of death, before the organs begin to atrophy. So with each client, we have a support team waiting in place. We send our team ahead of time, when the family lets us know that the end is imminent. The team members will wait, sometimes a week or more if that's what it takes. It's part of the package. As soon as the client is pronounced legally dead, the support team comes in and brings the body temperature down as quickly as possible."

213

"How do they do that, exactly?" Mohit sounds increasingly skeptical every time he opens his mouth.

"We cover the body in crushed ice, plus some water. A hose works to spray water across the patient; that accelerates the cooling process. And this"—he points to the blue pump on the demo body's chest—"this pump here keeps the heart pumping and oxygen flowing through the body."

"So the person is still alive, then? Her heart is pumping?"

"Mo," I say, a warning.

Dr. Fitzspelt doesn't look put off by Mohit's questions, though. "Her heart has stopped naturally at the moment of death. We restart it manually, with the pump. But if we shut down the pump, the heart stops again."

Mohit swallows, hard. "Oh. Right."

"The client is kept in this state while the body temperature is brought down. In that time, she's also given various medications—we use heparin to keep the blood from clotting, for example. This is all phase one. It happens right at the client's bedside."

"And it has to happen immediately?" Chloe chimes in.

"Yes," Dr. Fitzspelt answers. "Otherwise the process doesn't work. Preservation begins at the precise moment death is declared."

That hangs in the room for a moment. Maybe the three of us are all imagining the same moment. What is it like, *the* moment? Will I hurt, or will it be a relief from pain? Will I stink up the room with my smell of death, as I exhale my last putrid breaths over my unbrushed teeth and cotton tongue? Will they have to tear my mother away from me in the middle of her tears? Will she have time to say goodbye before I'm literally put on ice?

After a pause that feels longer than it probably is, Dr. Fitzspelt clears his throat. "Once the body is cooled, we transfer the client to our facility. That's when we begin the vitrification process." He stops there and looks at me closely. "Is this a bit too much, Astrid? I have all this information in writing."

"I think we'd like to get it in writing," Mohit says.

It irks me a little that he's speaking for me. At the same time, I *do* want it in writing. My head is swimming right now, partly from the influx of sobering information and partly with a general feeling of cloudiness. My lower back is starting to scream for a painkiller and a heating pad. I know I can't stay on my feet like this much longer without needing a break.

"Should we go upstairs, then? I'll give you the paperwork and information to take home, and you can think this all over."

We exit the elevator on the second floor, and the light of day pours in through windowed corridors, sending a sharp jab through my head, just behind my eyes. I blink it away.

"These are our labs, on this floor. And our offices. Here we go."

Just as he's about to open the door, it swings in the other

direction and Dr. Carl Vanderwalk, the Doogie Howser of cryonics, emerges. He looks surprised and then pleased to see me.

"Ah, Astrid Ayeroff, regular human! I was hoping I'd run into you while you were here. How are you?"

"Still kicking." I introduce him to Mohit and Chloe.

"Dr. Vanderwalk is our associate medical director," says Dr. Fitzspelt. "And one of the most promising new doctors in the field."

Carl brushes him off. "Stop, you're making me blush. I'm just doing my job. Well, you enjoy the rest of your tour. And, Astrid?" He takes my hand and looks me straight in the eye with his own piercing blue ones. His palm is cool but a little clammy with sweat. "Best of luck to you. Whatever you decide to do with the end of your present life, trust your gut. You'll make the right choices for you."

"Uh, thanks?" I'm unsure how else to respond, and take my hand back.

Dr. Fitzspelt clears his throat and ushers us into a standard-issue office. There's a cubicle by the door, occupied by a middle-aged white woman with an obvious line of caked-on foundation tracing her jaw. She smiles broadly at us and gestures toward a platter of doughnuts at the edge of her desk. "Hi there! Help yourselves. Dr. F., a few messages for you on your desk."

"Thank you, Charlene. Right this way, my friends."

I eye the doughnuts as we walk past, an assortment of glazed and powdered and chocolate frosted with rainbow sprinkles. Bright red jelly oozes from the center of one. My stomach turns.

We follow Dr. Fitzspelt into the inner office, which looks out over the parking lot and, beyond that, the rusty landscape Sedona is famous for. The doctor's workspace is so cluttered that it makes me wonder what his house looks like, and whether he might be a bona fide hoarder. There are piles of papers stacked high enough that I'm not sure I could see the little man if he was sitting behind them, along with coffee cups of varying sizes, books, yellow legal pads, old copies of *Scientific American*, and a half-eaten glazed doughnut on a napkin. I spy a familiar tote bag from the neuroscience symposium and three of the brain-shaped stress balls. He clears papers off three chairs and motions for us to sit down. Then he makes a space in front of his own chair and starts pulling up something or other on the screen of an ancient desktop PC.

"All right, then." Dr. Fitzspelt exhales deeply and grins at us. "It's such a pleasure to have young people here, I can't tell you. We really do believe this is the future of science, you see. But it's mostly us oldies working here. I do have a few, um, what do they call you all now—millennials? A few young-sters, anyway, working in the lab. You met Dr. Vanderwalk already, of course."

"Dr. Fitzspelt," Chloe interrupts, "do you mind if we do a quick interview with you on camera? For Astrid's vlog?"

"Her what? I'm sorry."

"Her video blog. It's a website we're using to raise the money for her cryopreservation. She has lots of followers—they

217

just want to know what the process is like. I'm sure they'd love to hear from you. It could be good publicity for the institute, too."

I've gotta hand it to Chloe, she would make a good agent.

"Oh, well, I suppose, yes." Dr. Fitzspelt sits up a little straighter in his chair, looking rather enthused about the idea of an interview. "We have been featured on the news quite a few times, as a matter of fact. I know I have DVDs of the clips around here somewhere . . ." He trails off as he starts scanning the area around his desk.

"That's okay, but it'd be great if we could get some original footage." Chloe holds up the camera bag. "Do you mind?"

Within minutes, she's got the tripod set up and Dr. Fitzspelt is sitting in front of it, his cluttered desk in full view. Chloe makes me sit in the shot, too, so my "fans" can see that I'm here in person with him.

"Okay," she says. "Ask him a few basic questions, Astrid."

"We already asked him the basic questions."

"Ask them again, then. Don't be difficult."

My head is throbbing now; I'm ready for a nap and some water. But I train my focus on Dr. Fitzspelt and force a smile at him.

"So a lot of people have been asking me, you know, is this possible? I guess that's my big question, too. Is it possible?"

The doctor chuckles, like he's telling himself a private joke about these "people" and their "questions."

"Of course, we hear that a lot, too, as you can imagine," he says. "Astrid, the thing is, this is *already* happening. Just recently—I don't know if you saw this on the news—a young man's body was recovered from under a snowbank where he had been trapped. Now, he had been dead for about twenty-four hours by the time he was found—that's what his doctors said. Really dead, no heartbeat, no brain activity, all right? Dead. But those doctors were able to warm his blood and *bring him back to life in the hospital.* Cryopreservation relies on the same science. What we're really doing here is simply learning how to take advantage of a process that already occurs in nature. If the body is brought to a sufficiently low temperature at the time of death, it opens all kinds of possibilities for revival."

I think about that. "So then . . . if that's the case, do you view cryopreservation as the act of reviving a dead person—or saving a life?"

Dr. Fitzspelt looks like he's taken off guard by the question. He scratches his chin for a moment and stares into the distance. "There are different schools of thought on this, Astrid. I can only tell you what I believe. We're not saving lives, per se. But the process does take advantage of the scientific reality of what happens in the moments immediately surrounding a natural death. Death isn't a single moment. It's a process."

Next to me, I sense Mohit tense up. I can practically hear the voice in his head screaming, Except it *is* a moment. But I like Dr. Fitzspelt's description. Because if dying is a process, then there must be multiple ways to do it well.

"Of course," Dr. Fitzspelt continues without anyone

asking him a follow-up, "bodies that have died from natural causes are, in many cases, diseased in ways that cannot be cured with *today's* medical science. But there's no reason that that will still be true a decade or two or three down the road. Your brain tumor, for example, could be cured with, say, genetic medicine or advances in surgery."

I try to imagine a world in which the astrocytoma blossoming in my skull and twisting its way irreparably around my healthy brain tissue could be someone else's nuisance, a literal and figurative headache to be cured with some pills or an outpatient surgery. It sends a surge of anger through me. Why not now? Why not me?

But then, perhaps, that's exactly Dr. Fitzspelt's point. If they preserve my body, it could be me. In a "now" I can't even comprehend.

I just wonder what that now will be like. Who *I'll* be, yes, but more important, who everyone else will be. Let's say it takes thirty years. Mohit will be middle-aged. He could be married to someone—someone very much alive—and have kids of his own. My mother could be a grandmother; my little brother, someone's dad. Liam'll barely even remember his once-dying sister. If the future of science can actually wake me up and make me healthy again, or at a very minimum bring back some piece of my consciousness, what world will I be coming back to?

★

"Is there anything else I can answer for you today?" Dr. Fitzspelt asks after Chloe has turned off the camera. He's looking at me intently, as if he's studying me.

I shake my head. "I don't think so. I mean, I might have some more questions later."

He nods curtly. "Of course, anytime. You have my information."

"I still have a question," Mohit says.

Leave it to Mo to be full of questions until the very last opportunity. Dr. Fitzspelt shifts his gaze to Mohit and waits.

"You keep saying maybe this, maybe that. This all seems, at best, unlikely."

Dr. Fitzspelt starts to interject, but Mohit continues.

"So what I'm wondering is, Is there anything you can do—or we can do—to up Astrid's chances of the procedure working? Like, in her particular case? I understand that we don't have any guarantees, but if we're going to go down this path . . ." He leaves the rest of his sentence hanging in midair.

Dr. Fitzspelt narrows his eyes a bit as he first takes in Mohit's face, then mine.

"Well," he says, then stops there. After what feels like a long pause, he parts his lips and waits still another moment before speaking. "There is one thing I would call a *possibility*. Something we're in talks about. But it's not part of our standard procedure at this time. I did think . . . Well, I wondered, when I heard from you, if you might be a good

221

candidate for this. But I don't want to pressure you, of course."

Mohit is frowning now.

"What is that?" I ask.

Dr. Fitzspelt stands up suddenly, a few papers drifting from his desk to the office floor. "Come with me, please. And please, I must ask that you keep what you're about to see confidential, as we are still in the development phase."

We follow him back down the hallway to the elevators, and then all the way to the very lowest level, a floor deeper than we've gone before. He doesn't say anything as he takes us down, and we don't ask any more questions.

Down the corridor, we reach a door that requires Dr. Fitzspelt's key card and fingerprint ID to enter. The heavy door swings open automatically after his prints are approved, and he motions us through it. On the other side, there are several more laboratory doors on either side of the hallway. Dr. Fitzspelt stops in front of one.

"This is our latest research. We don't offer this to current clients because we have yet to test this process in humans."

My mouth goes instantly dry; my stomach churns. "What process?"

He presses his fingertips to another ID pad, then motions us into the room after him. It's the kind of laboratory I've seen a hundred times in movies—a cramped, windowless room with several rows of cages, packed on top of each other and labeled with numerical codes. It's cold in the room, even colder than the labs upstairs. And all around us, the quiet, persistent squeaking of rats.

I shiver as we follow Dr. Fitzspelt to the farthermost row of cages.

"What is all this?" Mohit asks. I can tell from the low vibration of his voice that he's not happy.

"This is our most compelling possibility." Dr. Fitzspelt runs a long, thin finger along the edge of the first cage, where a white rat with tiny red eyes scurries around industriously. "This rat, and the others in this row here, have all been previously cryopreserved."

We take that in for a moment. They look like active, squeaking rats. Except at some point, they've been frozen. "So they were, basically, dead?" I ask.

"They were."

"And now they're alive?"

Dr. Fitzspelt nods. "These rats are part of a new phase of our research that has indicated to us that we can achieve quite . . . let me say, quite remarkable results, provided we take certain steps *prior* to cryopreservation."

Mohit shifts from one foot to the other. "And what are those steps? Clearly you're getting at something, Doctor. Do you want to tell us what it is?"

I jab him in the waist. Dr. Fitzspelt is giving us the insider treatment here. The last thing we need is him suddenly deciding we're just obnoxious teenagers. But if Dr. Fitzspelt's irritated, his face doesn't give it away. Instead, he just stares at us, his eyes gleaming and shifting from one of us to the next. Finally, they land on me.

"I told you the story of the young man whose body was found frozen in the woods, yes?"

Three nods: me, Mohit, Chloe.

"Well, these rats have that in common, to a certain extent, with that young man."

Next to me, Mohit is getting impatient, I can tell. "In that . . . ?"

"In that these rats were also frozen before their clinical deaths. Or, put more plainly, we accelerated their deaths, in order to begin the preservation process in the moments before, rather than the moments after, their hearts stopped."

None of us says anything. I'm not sure what to say, frankly. I stare at the rats, white, beady-eyed. *Alive.* Revived. Raised from the dead.

Except they weren't dead, not to begin with. That's the point.

We sit across from Dr. Fitzspelt at his desk once more. This time, the three of us are even more lost for words than we were an hour ago. Mohit keeps shaking his head and looking up at the ceiling like he knows that what he's thinking would be inappropriate to say.

I search for the right words to form just one of the many questions swirling in my head. "So, if the procedure has a better chance of working if you—"

"Let me stop you there," Dr. Fitzspelt says, cutting in. "We can't say that for sure. As I said, this is early-stage research. It's a theory, really, that we're currently testing on animals."

"You're killing animals by freezing them to death, in order to test whether or not you can wake them up again?" Mohit practically spits the question.

"That's . . . not exactly how I would put it."

"How else would you put it? These animals were alive, right? They weren't *actually dying* and then frozen at the moment of their natural death. That's what you told us would happen to Astrid if she goes through with this procedure. Now you're saying, what? She has a better chance of being revived one day if you . . . *kill* her by freezing her?"

"Mo," I say under my breath, putting a hand on his arm. He pulls away.

"I understand your confusion," Dr. Fitzspelt says patiently. "Let me explain better. The process—which again, to date, has not been tested on a human—is not that death takes place via freezing. What we were able to do with the rats was to begin the process of lowering their body temperatures prior to death. Then, in effect, we stopped their hearts artificially, once their bodies were already cool."

"And in a human, you would call that . . . what?" Mo asks.

I swallow. I know what I would call it. I also know that it's not legal in Massachusetts.

"Euthanasia?" I say, barely audible.

Chloe jerks her head toward me. "Assisted suicide?"

Dr. Fitzspelt stammers, clearly unraveling. "It's—it's not euthanasia, per se. No, no. It's . . . we're—"

"It is," Mo says firmly. "You're looking for a person who's dying, like Astrid, but instead of waiting until she's *actually* dead to preserve her body, you want to preemptively start the process and kill her before she otherwise would die. And assuming she's given you permission to do that, as far as I understand it, that means you want to assist in her suicide. That's what that is."

"That is a very *misguided* way of looking at this." Dr. Fitzspelt turns away from Mohit and makes eye contact with me. "Astrid, the people who come to us for cryopreservation—they're like you. They're dreamers. They're hopeful. They want to write their own stories, choose their own approach to the end of their present lives. You are young. Your heart is healthy. Based on our research, you could be an excellent candidate for this next era of preservation and revitalization. Of course, I welcome you to join our program under our standard package, which I do believe stands a good chance of success down the road. But this new approach is . . ." He pauses there, licks the fine film of spit from his lips. "This is our best chance of success. It is the future of science."

Those words, again.

Mohit pushes his chair away from the desk, stands up, and holds his hand out for me. "Astrid, we should go."

He practically drags me across the parking lot. Chloe trails behind us, trying to snap some pictures of the exterior of the institute on her phone before we leave without her. It's only then, as we beeline for the Tomato, that the end of *Charlie and the Chocolate Factory* pops into my brain: Willie Wonka turns out to be kind of a sad old man. Lonely, wistful, and desperate for some child who might want to carry on his legacy.

40.

AT FIRST, WE'RE QUIET IN THE TOMATO, JUST
the hum of the engine serving as muted road-trip music as we
get back on the road.

The future of science. Our best chance of success.

I roll Dr. Fitzspelt's words over and over in my head,
thinking about what they mean in practical terms. I'm already dying. What difference would it make, really, if I died a
few weeks or a few months earlier than I would anyway, if it
meant a better chance of waking up again one day, of meeting
Liam's future children, of hearing grown-up Mohit play his
saxophone in those swanky jazz clubs?

"We didn't have to rush out of there like that," I say finally. "It was rude."

"Rude?" Mohit is still seething. "You know what's rude,
Astrid? Bringing us out there for a visit on the pretense of offering a program to freeze your body after your death, only
to spring on us that he's eyeing you as a guinea pig for some
underground thing where he takes you from us before you're

actually ready to die, in the interest of furthering his research. Which, by the way, is still highly unlikely to work. And you'd be killing yourself. No. Just no. Never mind the animal testing, which is cruel to begin with."

"You asked him, Mo! He was just answering your question. I don't see how you can really blame him for that. Who knows if he even would've mentioned the other thing if you hadn't asked."

Chloe glances at me in the rearview mirror. "It was kind of creepy, though. I mean, there's a reason they're not offering that, um, service to the general public. It'd be illegal in most states."

"Right. Which is my point—he wasn't even going to mention it. I think you're both being too hard on the poor guy."

"The poor guy," Mohit grumbles. "Right."

"Anyway, it's definitely illegal in Massachusetts, because of that ballot initiative from a few years ago," Chloe adds. "Although I think that was kind of misguided of our voters, don't you?"

I still remember the headlines, when the initiative was on the ballot in Massachusetts, and the woman whose name was all over the news, the poster child of the Death with Dignity campaign: Chiara Antony. In her forties, mother of two. She had ALS, Lou Gehrig's disease. There's no cure. She was losing her muscle function, but her brain was intact. She was becoming trapped in her own body, she knew it, and she wanted out.

She'd stuck with me, not because I had any idea at that point that I might be making the same decision, but because even then, when I still thought my own death was a far-off, eventual, by-the-time-I'm-sick-of-living-anyway thing, I thought, What is a human life if you're not allowed any agency in how you leave it?

My mother agreed, clucking her tongue at the television every time Chiara's face would come on the news. "This poor woman," she'd say. "She deserves the right to die on her own terms while she still can."

"Misguided?" Mo says. "Doctors are supposed to do no harm. It's kind of in their job description. I think it's fairly clear that helping someone kill themselves is causing harm. Plus it's just . . . interfering with the natural order of things."

There's a persistent ache in my hips and lower back, and my head still has that fuzzy, buzzing feeling I couldn't put my finger on earlier, only now it's louder than before. "Your definition of harm is rather narrow, though, don't you think? I mean, what if treatment itself is causing harm? What if a person has no quality of life? What if their wish is to end their life peacefully, on their own terms?"

No one says anything for a long moment. Mohit has shifted away from me, his face pressed against the Tomato's window. When he finally turns back to meet my eyes, his face is wet with tears.

Mohit never cries.

Or never that he lets me see.

"I'm not saying I'm going to do this," I say quietly. "I'm not saying anything. I'm just saying—people have the right to their choices."

He sighs. "Fine. Point taken. I just don't want you to put your hopes in this thing—this procedure, whatever you want to call it—so much that you miss out on everything you could be enjoying while you're still here. It could be a huge sham."

"You're not talking about *my* hopes, though, are you? Because if it does turn out to be a sham, I'll never know."

Mohit's cheeks redden, and his eyes get glossy again.

I go on. "Really, it's *your* hopes you're talking about. You don't want to put *your* hopes in this."

He shrugs and looks away.

"But you could be dead by the time I wake up, too! Or you could be seventy years old, in which case, Mo, you're not going to care anymore. You're going to have moved on. Everyone will have moved on, except me. I'll still be sixteen."

"Seventeen," Chloe says softly from behind the wheel. "Your birthday is coming up."

"Seventeen. Whatever. My point is, this isn't anyone's call but mine, because by the time the possibility is even remotely plausible, you'll all have long forgotten me anyway."

"Screw you, Astrid."

He says it so quietly I almost can't hear him. Except I can, and it stings.

"Chloe, pull over," he says more loudly.

"Huh?"

"Please pull over."

I hear the click of the Tomato's blinker, and Chloe maneuvers us to the shoulder and stops the engine. Mohit moves far faster than I possibly can. He hops down the stairs and onto the road.

By the time I manage to follow him, he's stalked angrily out onto the desert land by the side of the road. He settles himself onto a low, red rock, staring in the opposite direction from the highway. I go to him slowly, touch his shoulder.

He doesn't turn or even react at all at first. His face is damp.

"Sorry," I mumble.

Mo shakes his head firmly but doesn't say anything.

"I said I was sorry."

He swallows. The pulse of that Adam's apple makes my heart swell.

"You're right, Astrid. It is about me. And your mother. And Chloe. And Liam. It is about the people who love you. Because we're the ones who will be left behind to live with an Astrid-shaped hole in the universe. We don't want to lose you before we have to. And it isn't fair to ask us to."

I sit on a rock next to him. Neither of us speaks. What does an Astrid-shaped hole look like? I picture an Astrid cutout in the earth's atmosphere, like the outline of a body on the ground at a crime scene, only me, breaking my way out of civilization, out of the universe, into whatever is beyond it.

Eventually, Mo gets to his feet, dusts the red earth from his jeans, and lumbers back toward the Tomato. I follow him.

41.

WE DON'T SAY ANYTHING ELSE AS WE PASS
through the outskirts of Sedona. As the signs of the city start
to dissipate and the long highway stretches out beyond us, we
pass a sign for Red Rock State Park. Five miles.

"Let's stop," I say.

Mohit's resting his head against the back of the bench seat
opposite me. Now he opens his eyes but doesn't move. "Stop
for what?" He's still sore from our argument, I can tell.

"Aren't we on a road trip of great Americana? May as well
take advantage of what's in front of us. Plus, there's probably
a bathroom."

We park near a visitor center with curved walls built of
uneven red bricks and low, beamed ceilings. At the gate, a
woman in a vest takes our entrance fees. She hastily prints
three tickets and hands them to Mohit, tucked in a folded
map. "Trails are marked in your map, no going off-trail. Park
closes at five o'clock."

I glance at my phone: it's just past two.

When Chloe and I come out of the visitor center bathroom, Mohit is studying the map. "I think we should take this one here, Smoke Trail." He runs his finger along a blue dotted line.

"That's the shortest one," I say, taking the map from his hands.

I can feel a look passing between him and Chloe. Neither says anything.

"Here: the Eagle's Nest Overlook is the highest point in the park," I say. "That's where we're going."

Without waiting for them, I head off in the direction of the trail entrances, marked by a set of colored signs.

"Astrid," Mo says, coming after me. It doesn't take much effort for him to catch up. His face is set in a hard, frustrated line. "Can you not be ridiculous right now?"

I whirl around. "Oh? How am I being ridiculous?"

"We're not going to do the longest, hardest trail in the park. Be realistic."

I'm about to fight him harder, but I think better of it. When I look from him to Chloe, she's pleading with me, too, red-faced and biting her bottom lip. They came all this way for me, not just the physical trip but the emotional one. To respect my choices. Which is exactly what I've been wanting, really: some say in how all this goes down.

I soften my tone. "What if we just go a little bit toward Eagle's Nest? If I'm not feeling up to it, we'll stop."

They exchange a glance. Then Mo sighs, and puts his arm through mine.

The earth leaves rusty orange dust on our sneakers as we wind our way along the Eagle's Nest Loop, along a trail lined with short green shrubbery and things that look like cacti, but what do I know. The sun is past its peak, but we still warm up quickly as we walk. I peel off my sweatshirt almost immediately and curse myself for putting it on in the first place.

"Hold on a sec." I perch on a rock on the trail's edge.

Mo hands me his water, looking desperate to say "I told you so." I know that's what he's thinking. We've been walking for all of ten minutes, and I already need a break.

"Okay?" he asks as I tip a few small sips toward the back of my throat. If I drink too much, we'll run out. Plus, I doubt there are any bathrooms along the Eagle's Nest Loop, and I'm not really one for squatting in the brush.

Chloe shields her eyes with one hand and looks out over the park. In the near-ish distance, more piles of red rock rise up against the horizon, dotted with greenery. I wonder what view is waiting for us from the highest point in the park. We have to get there.

I pass the bottle back to Mohit, and he helps me to my feet again.

We follow the trail in a slowly rising loop around the park. It's not too steep, fortunately, and if I take a break every few minutes to catch my breath and sip some water, it's manageable. Mohit finds me a branch along the side of the trail and I lean on it as I walk, which helps me ignore the throbbing that's progressively radiating from my head to my temples and down my spine. We don't say much as we walk. Mostly, I'm focused on the rusty ground in front of me, one step at a time, and sucking as much dry, desert air into my lungs as I can.

Finally, we round a sloping corner, and just up ahead can see the trail's summit, a rolling ledge of red rocks. I force myself forward to the very top and throw the walking stick down at my feet in triumph.

Beyond us, the park stretches out in acres of warmth in every direction. Straight across from where we stand, two huge side-by-side rock formations look like those drip castles I used to make at the beach when I was little, the kind where you take the wettest sand and let it slip from your clasped hand. One is an almost perfectly cylindrical tower that looks not unlike a natural-world version of the capsules in Dr. Fitzspelt's lab. Its neighbor to the right is larger and more irregular, with a sloped top and ridges running up and down its body, so it looks like it's made of thin slices of rock collapsed together.

It's nothing I've ever seen before, the view from up here. It's the perfect complement to the view from Lucy's belly: an altogether otherworldly landscape, everything from the smells to the colors to the sound of the wind distinct from the coast, but right here on this same land mass.

The view burns into my memory, mine for as long as I have memories.

I lean against a boulder, taking the weight off my lower

back. My legs have gone nearly numb. Mohit sidles up next to me and slips an arm around my shoulder without saying anything.

I press my cheek to his sleeve. "Are you still mad?"

He shrugs. "Maybe a little." Neither of us looks at the other. Instead, we both stare out over the land below us, our eyes collecting the same images, or maybe different ones. He smells slightly sweaty. As close as we are, I can feel a chasm opening between us, the one that's probably inevitable between a person whose life is fading and a person whose life is really just beginning.

"I wanted to see the view from up here," I say. "I want to see as many views as I can."

I feel his body rise and fall with his breath. "I know."

"Smile!" Chloe's pointing her phone at us. Wrapped against his chest, I can feel Mo smiling, which makes me smile, too. But the buzzing in my head is louder than ever, and the numbness creeping through my back and legs says something isn't right, in a new way.

"I just want to say this one thing, and then I'll shut up," Mohit says.

"Okay."

"Okay. Here's what scares me. What scares me is that you'll take Dr. Fitzspelt's offer, and you'll want to charge ahead with it, even though the clinical trial is still a real possibility. And you'll just give in to the tumor." When he finally meets my eyes, he looks more hurt than mad. I put a hand to his cheek, which he hasn't shaved since we left Boston. The dark stubble has grown into almost a beard in the few days we've been gone.

"The trial won't work."

"You don't know that. You don't."

"It will wreck me to try."

"Again, you don't know that."

I sigh. There's nothing I can say to convince him of what I know in my bones, which is that no matter what new treatment gets thrown my way, my body is ready to be finished.

"Mo, I just want to do this my way."

"What does that mean, though?"

"It means that whatever I decide, *I* want to decide. And I want you to be okay with it."

He looks out over the landscape in front of us. I'm used to waiting through Mohit's thinking silences. But as the quiet moments tick by, this starts to feel like a long silence, even for him.

Finally, he lets out a deep, long exhale. "I love you, Astrid Ayeroff. I'm afraid of my life without you." He squeezes me tighter to his chest. "But we've come this far. Whatever you choose now, I have to be okay with it."

I blink away tears. "I love you, Mohit Parikh. I'm sorry for leaving you. And thank you."

42.

And then, just like that.
Everything.
Goes.
Black.

43.

Beep.
Ping.
Chirp.
Beep.
Ping.
Chirp.

44.

MY THROAT IS COATED IN SANDPAPER. MY
eyelids are weighed down with magnets.

That's how it feels to wake up here.

Foreign, and familiar.

45.

"HI, BABY. HI, MY LOVE. ARE YOU AWAKE?"

My mother, soft and sleepy, gradually comes into focus in my field of vision. She looks hazy around the edges, between my blurred eyesight and her mussed hair, the sleep-encrusted corners of her eyes.

"Hi."

"Here," she says, putting a straw to my lips. The water feels good. I suck down as much as I can.

"How long have I been . . . whatever this is?"

"It's been a week, love. You had a seizure, and then they put you in an induced coma for the first three days. Since then you've been in and out. You're fine now."

Fine.

Fine.

The word sounds laughable in my head, like it's not even a real word.

As the room comes into view around me, I see the usual signs of "fine": the recliner with faux-leather cushions where my mother has probably been sleeping for days. The dry-erase board with drawings of faces from happy to sad—"How's your pain on a scale of one to ten?" The IVs embedded in the backs of my hands, connecting me to hanging bags of fluids. The flat-screen television, news on a loop, muted. The bathroom door cracked open. The beeping monitor, the flashing green numbers indicating my heart rate, my oxygen levels—numbers that always define us but go unnoticed until they demand attention.

But the view out the window is unfamiliar. There's an Applebee's sign rising up over a highway. Beyond that, red rolling hills. It makes me feel a touch Dorothy-ish, but without the yappy dog, waking up in a landscape I don't recognize.

Mom must see me looking.

"We're still in Arizona, babe."

"Where are . . ." I want to ask more questions, but my mouth won't cooperate.

"They went home, my love. I'm sorry. School and everything."

I try to imagine Chloe and Mohit driving the Tomato back east without me. The long stretches of silence, filled by the radio. I wonder what they listened to: Did Mohit let Chloe play Top 40 the whole way just to avoid a fight? They probably didn't stop at any more of the sights in *The Top 50 Roadside Attractions*. Though I almost like to imagine that they did, just the two of them. My two favorites, taking in the world's largest ball of twine together.

"You'll be out of here soon, once you're cleared to fly," Mom says. "Okay?"

"Out of here soon" means home to Dr. Klein's office, to my friendly neighborhood hospital. I know that once the seizures start, they generally don't end. It probably means my cancer has grown, taken its own road trip to visit my better-functioning organs. Like I knew it would. I don't feel panicked, though. Instead, I feel something more like a sense of relief. Like something that seemed really complicated for a long time is suddenly made clear.

Mom lays her palm on my cheek. Her warm hand on my skin relaxes my body. My mother is here. For a moment, I really am fine.

"Mom?" My voice is barely above a squeak as my vocal cords wake up after a week of silence.

"Yes, my love?" She leans closer to me. "Don't strain your voice, Astrid."

"Mom. I don't want this anymore."

A smile flashes across her face for an instant, more like an involuntarily impulse than an indication of happiness. "What's 'this,' my love?"

"Hospitals. Chemo. The trial. I don't want any more stuff. I want to go home."

Her face is immobile for a moment. Then she stands up abruptly, flustered, and feels my forehead. "I think your fluids are running low. I'll get the nurse."

46.

I CAN'T GET OUT OF BED ON MY OWN, BUT IT doesn't matter. I don't need to. All I need is my phone and the password to the hospital's wifi.

When my mother has gone for lunch and the nurse has just been in to take my vitals and re-up my pain meds, I figure I have a few minutes to myself—rare, in a hospital. I take out my phone and flip the lens to face myself.

Then, when I'm done, I go to YouTube, sign in as Chloe, and upload the new video.

47.

I WANT TO DIE. I MEAN, I DON'T WANT TO
die. I want to live, actually, but I don't have that choice in front of
me. I do have a choice about dying. I want to do it my way.

I'm sure you know by now, since you've been watching these videos, that I have a high-grade astrocytoma. I'm in the hospital at the
moment because I had a pretty bad seizure while I was on my way
back from visiting the American Institute for Cryonics Research. I
don't know how much longer I'll live. But I do know that it won't be
long enough not to miss out on all the things I don't want to miss.

I thought I wanted to cryopreserve myself after my death, so
maybe I wouldn't have to miss everything. You know that. That's why
you're watching. Maybe you even gave me money to help me do that,
and I really appreciate it. But one thing I realized when I visited the
institute is that I'm going to miss things, whether I wake up forty
years from now or not. Missing things is kind of inevitable.

I guess that probably sounds obvious. The thing is, researching
cryopreservation offered me something to do about dying. Cancer when
you're sixteen feels like a joke. It's not like a real thing you can wrap

your head around. And you can do all the treatments they throw at you, but at the end of the day cancer does what cancer wants. Dr. Fitzspelt offered me a choice—a way to have a say in the end of my life—when no one else was offering me one. And that's really all I want.

Now that I'm back here in this hospital bed, I remember what all this is like. Not that you forget, really, but it sort of loses its sharpness when you've been in basically pretty good shape again for a while. Now I remember everything I don't want the rest of my life to be. I don't want to be in doctors' offices. I don't want to be in clinical trials. But I don't want to freeze my body either. I don't want strangers in lab coats hanging around, prodding me, waiting for me to kick it. I don't want to feel like I'm dying on someone else's clock. I just want to die—on my terms, in my time.

So I'm choosing now to treat my pain only. They can do that, you know—just make you comfortable, make your pain manageable without trying to fix things that won't be fixed. And when I'm near the end, I plan to stop eating and drinking to make the process go faster, so I don't suffer. And so my family doesn't suffer, any more than they have to. I intend to write an advance directive and share it with my parents, and I'm going to trust them to help me execute it.

That's what I want. The money you've donated will go to pediatric brain cancer research, by the way. I want to be part of the future of science, and that's a better way to do it. Cryopreservation is a long shot, but these treatment advances are real. Maybe I'll have to miss everything, but some other kid won't. So don't worry—I'm not just going to spend it, like, buying fancy shit in my last few months alive. Anyway, thanks for listening.

Uh, over and out.

48.

SUNLIGHT BOUNCES OFF A TINY CRYSTAL
pendant someone affixed to the window, sending a smattering
of rainbows across the wall. Under normal circumstances, I
would've complained about someone hanging a crystal in my
room, but I can't muster the energy to be snarky. And rainbows are pretty.

I text Mo with a link to the new video.

Okay?

I send a similar message to Chloe, since I know she'll see
the video as soon as she checks our vlog channel.

A few minutes go by, with nothing. Then my phone
buzzes.

It's a sad-face emoji from Mo. He uses the man emoji
with light brown skin and dark hair, which always makes
me laugh because the hair is way too short for him and it's
impossible to imagine him looking so clean-cut in real life.
Today, it makes tears well up in my eyes. It's absurd, an
emoji from my boyfriend in response to the news that I've

posted my intent to die to the internet. Absurd, but also kind of perfect.

Then my phone buzzes again. Actual words this time.

Okay. Like I promised.

I let out a breath I didn't know I'd been holding.

49.

YOU KNOW HOW, THANKS TO THE INTERNET,
people can go from being mostly just normal to being Really
Kind of a Big Deal overnight? People on reality television and
whatnot. I always sort of wondered if they felt like they'd gone
down a rabbit hole—if they woke up one morning and read
near-fiction about themselves online and thought, "The world
is not as I thought it was."

Turns out, yeah. That's pretty much how it is.

When I wake up the next morning, my latest video—my
last video, presumably—has been shared on Reddit. Once it's
on Reddit, it's off and running, and I can't take it back.

So this kid was collecting money to save her life, and
now she wants to die? Do we think she even has
cancer? Seems like a sham to me.

I donated for Astrid's future resurrection, not her
suicide. Where is my money?

Is there a money-back guarantee on this nutjob?

Where r her parents?

What did you do? Chloe texts. *Why didn't you discuss this with me first?*

I call her. "It was an impulse. I tried to talk to my mom, and it didn't go well."

On the other end of the phone, I hear Chloe typing something. Multitasking. "And this was your response?"

"I guess."

She clears her throat. "Well. If you wanted to call attention to your cause, it's working."

Is that what I wanted to do? I don't even know what "my cause" is. The vlog started as a way to raise some money. Granted, it was an uncomfortable way to raise money, but as Chloe has pointed out multiple times, asking for help on the internet is pretty standard these days. She showed me crowdfunding pages set up to send college students abroad, to buy groceries, to make movies, to bury newborns who never made it home. But gradually, my videos had started to feel like something different, like a way to tell secrets into the void, to sort out how I was feeling, out loud. I almost forgot the audience was even there.

I click through more of the comments, which grow in number every time I refresh the page.

Cancer kid is pretty cute tho. I'd do her before she kicks it.

Or after. LOL.

I close the page.

"Astrid?" Chloe's still on the phone. "You want me to take this down? You know it won't really go away, though, even if I do, right?"

I shake my head but then realize she can't see me over the phone. "It's okay. Leave it."

50.

"KNOCK KNOCK? CAN I COME IN?" DAD SAYS, poking his head into the room.

I put my phone aside and try to erase the voices of the internet-commenting public from my head. "Hey, Dad."

I didn't know it at the time, of course, but my father got to the hospital first, before Mom, since he had the geographic advantage. He must've rented a car, though it wouldn't entirely surprise me if he had biked here all the way from the Ranch.

"Good to see you awake, my girl. You scared us."

"Sorry." *Us.* It's a strange word, coming from him. I know he means him and Mom, even though they're not a unit anymore.

Dad hovers awkwardly. He looks around and catches a glimpse of the twinkling rainbows bouncing off the floor and walls. "Nice, huh?"

"Um, sure."

"The crystal's from Suzanne. She sent it with me—she wanted you to have a little joy in here."

Go figure. "Tell her thanks from me."

"I will. Look, I wanted to tell you the good news, now that you're in better shape. You have a sister, as of three days ago. Alice."

A sister, born while I was in the darkness of a coma. "Alice Ayeroff," I say, rolling her name around in my mouth.

"Turner-Ayeroff, hyphenated, actually. But yes. Do you want to see a picture?" He takes a photo from his pocket—a real, hard-copy photograph; I wonder where you can even get one printed near the Ranch—and offers it gently. "That was the day she was born."

She's a tiny, pink thing, swaddled in white muslin, barely human, just a squishy face with crystalline gray-blue eyes. She looks a lot like I did in my baby pictures.

"She's beautiful."

He nods. "She looks like you."

"You remember what I looked like?"

Dad's face contorts, and for a split second I see that I've hurt him. "Astrid, of course I do."

He's caused me pain over the years, first by leaving, then by blaming me for my own illness. But it doesn't feel good to hurt him back.

I hand him the photo. "Congrats, Dad. I'm happy for you both. All three of you." And I am, I think.

"Thank you." He looks at the picture for another moment, his face soft and affectionate. Then he puts it back in his shirt pocket hastily, as though he doesn't want to appear too focused on his new, healthy daughter while sitting here with his old, sick one. "So you visited the facility. What did you think of it? Do you remember much?"

I remember the rows of freezers, the strange fact of bodies encased in cold, hovering between life and death. Dr. Fitzspelt's offer to test his newest hypothesis on me. The possibility of choosing how and when I die. I can't even begin to describe it to my father. It's really the ultimate "you had to be there."

"Is Mom around?" I ask, not answering his question. I need to have a conversation with both of my parents, and since there isn't going to be a particularly good time to have it, I settle for now.

Dad looks relieved that I've offered him something to do. "I think so. You want me to go find her?" He hurries out into the hall.

When my parents appear as a pair in the doorway a moment later, though, Mom's face is completely devoid of color. She's holding her phone in her hand.

"Astrid." Her voice is dry and flat, almost shaking. "What did you do?"

There's a long moment in which the room—the whole world—feels at a standstill.

"A reporter just called me," Mom says. "From BuzzFeed? To ask for a comment on why I'm letting my child choose to hasten her own death. Am I letting my child hasten her own death, Astrid? Because that's news to me."

Mom's not crying. She's not even yelling. Her body language is screaming, but her voice holds steady. I can tell she's gone way beyond the normal range of angry, sad, scared. She's everything, all at once, and nothing at all.

"How could you do this?" She's speaking barely above a whisper now, full of hurt and rage and grief. The words barely escape her throat.

I don't know what I was expecting, but it wasn't to get scooped by BuzzFeed. I don't know what to say. Dad meanders to the corner and looks out the window at the Applebee's sign.

"Let me say that again." Mom gets louder. "How. Could. You."

"I tried to talk to you," I say. "But you wouldn't listen. I had to make it public. To make it real."

Suddenly, it's like my mother has woken up from a dream. She sends the facial-expression-equivalent of a torpedo right through my skull. "To make it *real*? What does that even mean, Astrid? This is your actual life we're talking about here, not some Facebook meme."

I'm so surprised by Mom's use of the word "meme" that I momentarily forget what we're really talking about.

"Maxine, maybe we should talk about this privately," Dad says coolly, cutting in.

"Why? It's my life," I say. "Why can't you discuss it with me?"

"Astrid!" My mother throws her phone on the bed. It bounces once, then careens off the other side and onto the floor with a clatter that's probably a cracked screen. No one moves to pick it up. "You have got to be kidding me right now! Do you hear what you're saying? Really hear yourself? Look at you right now. You're talking to us. You're breathing. You're eating. You're not in pain. You have life left in you! You're just going to give up on the trial? And you told the YouTube-viewing public that without any discussion? With Dr. Klein? With *your mother*? Do I get no say here?" Tears pour from her eyes now. "You are still alive!"

"Mom."

"And you want to throw that away? For what? For what? No. Absolutely not. You're my child. You're not—no."

"Okay, Max. Max." Dad crosses the room and puts a hand on my mother's shoulder. "Breathe. Breathe. Calm down for a moment."

"Calm down? Really, Richard? You're going to waltz in here and tell me to calm down about my daughter tossing around the idea of assisted suicide? Really?"

"It's not assisted suicide, Mom. It's palliative care. There's a big difference."

"The end result is the same, Astrid. It's my daughter, giving up on her life before she has to."

"She's my daughter, too," Dad says gently. "And I'd like to discuss this privately."

Mom throws her head back and laughs, practically guffaws, at the ceiling. It's a disconcerting, creepy laugh, throaty and unnatural, nothing like her. "Oh, that's perfect, Richard. She is your daughter, you're right. She's your daughter in one visit a year. She's your daughter in occasional phone calls. She's your daughter when you come sweeping into the hospital to play Superdad in an emergency. And now you want a say in this, too? Does everyone get a say except me, the person who brought her into this world and has kept her in it this long by fighting for every last goddamn possible cure?"

"Okay, guys." I close my eyes. "Guys."

"We're not having this discussion, Astrid. I'm sorry. No." When Mom shakes her head, her wild red curls spill across her shoulders. "No."

She storms out of the room.

Dad watches her go. "Well," he says finally. "Maybe it wasn't very fair of you to put this on the internet before talking to her about it first."

"I *tried*," I insist. But I can't fight over this anymore. My head hurts. Everything hurts. When my mother said I wasn't in pain, it should've been a question. She doesn't know.

51.

ONCE THE BUZZFEED STORY POPS UP, MY face—in a still from the video—starts appearing on the homepages of every internet gossip magazine I didn't know existed, all of which now seem deeply interested in my personal choices about life and death.

The headlines tell their own stories. "How Young Is Too Young to Choose to Die?" asks one opinion piece. "Parents Choose to End Medical Care for Terminally Ill Daughter," declares another, particularly inaccurately, since my parents have chosen no such thing and, as far as I can tell, haven't even agreed to let me go through with this. But in the court of the internet, they've already been judged and condemned.

These people have no right to call themselves parents. Parents are supposed to protect their kids at all costs. These people are doing anything but.

Murderers. They should go away for this. Ur gonna let your kid die? You should die too.

They'll pay, if not in this life, then in the next.

"It's a slow news cycle," Chloe says over the phone. She's trying to sound sage, but I can tell from the slight waver in her voice that this is unknown territory, even for my most internet-savvy friend. "They'll forget about you in a day or two."

They haven't yet, though.

I sigh. "Why does anyone care, anyway?"

"I mean, you made them care. They care because they think they know you."

But they don't know me. They don't know anything about me, except the carefully curated little slivers of myself I've offered them. They certainly don't know my parents. And now they think they have the whole story. Sour bile creeps up in my throat.

I stare at my own image on the screen. My little remaining hair is matted over my scalp. There's just the smallest bit of blue in the cancery wisps, through which the scar from my first brain surgery is visible again, a fine pink thread of tissue holding my skull together.

Hours go by, but my mother doesn't come back.

52.

LATE IN THE AFTERNOON, I CONVINCE MY
favorite nurse, a grandmotherly character named Celia, to
take me downstairs. It's the first time I've left this room since
I got here, and she helps me into my own loose sweatpants and
hoodie. It feels good to be clothed again. Almost human.
Being out of the hospital bed and in regular clothes gives me
a boost of confidence. I'm right. This is exactly why I'm making this choice.

Celia takes me on a wheelchair lap around the first-floor
lobby, where there's a gift shop and a café with boxed sandwiches and one of those machines that shoots out coffee *or*
cappuccino *or* a mocha *or* hot chocolate, all from the same
spout. There's no sign of Mom, though.

But then, just as we're headed back to the elevator, I spot
her through the window. I almost don't recognize her at first.
She's a stranger with curly hair, huddled on a bench outside
the emergency room entrance. Smoking a cigarette.

The automatic doors slide open, and the fresh air smells

like a mix of sunshine and warm weather and exhaust from the highway. And as the wind shifts, smoke. Celia wheels me over, and steps discreetly aside.

"Mom?" She notices me, then shifts her eyes away and lets out a heavy sigh. It's the first time I've ever registered my mother being not happy to see me.

"What are you doing?" I ask.

"What am I doing?"

"Since when do you smoke?"

She drops the half cigarette to the curb and snuffs it out with the heel of her sneaker. "We all get to make our choices, don't we, Astrid?" Her voice has a bitter edge to it that's as new to me as the image of my mother taking a drag off a Marlboro Light.

"I'm sorry I didn't talk to you again before I made the video," I blurt out.

"We've had that conversation before."

"I know. I'm sorry. But I did try, and you didn't really hear me."

"So now I'm Cruella De Vil of the internet? Bad Mom du Jour? That's what you wanted? Everyone to judge us, and me, so you'd get your way?"

The automatic doors slide open behind me, and a man comes out carrying a newborn in a car seat, his wife walking gingerly alongside them. He rests the car seat on the ground and unlocks the back door of an SUV parked with its lights flashing out front.

"Congratulations," Mom says. "Beautiful baby."

"Thank you." As he closes the door on his newborn, now

safely tucked away in the back seat, his eyes land on me. He smiles uncomfortably.

Your kid won't get cancer and die on you, I want to promise him. But I can't.

They drive away.

"I didn't want you to be judged," I say finally. "I wanted you to listen to me."

She doesn't say anything, just looks out over the parking lot and across the highway, where a magnificent landscape unfolds on the other side of a strip mall and high-rise condos.

"I get it, Mom. You want me to do the trial. But the trial isn't a solution. It isn't going to work."

"It definitely won't work if you don't enroll in it."

"Have you seen all this?" I gesture toward the rolling IV next to me, dripping fluids and pain meds into my veins. "It's not going anywhere. The trial is a Hail Mary. It's a shot in the dark. It's a fill-in-the-blank idiom meaning 'highly unlikely to work.'"

She doesn't respond. Her eyes are full of tears, but none of them escape down her cheeks.

I go on. "What the trial is highly likely to do, though, with almost one hundred percent certainty, is make me spend the last months of my life in treatment for something that refuses to be treated. That means more of *this*. And I don't want that. I can't control my cancer. This is a choice I can make. I can control this."

I pause there. I've started making some notes for my advance directive on my phone, following a form I downloaded from an organization that advocates for death-with-dignity laws. Voluntarily refusing to eat and drink is not considered assisted suicide. It's just a choice. But for a sixteen-year-old, any choice about medical treatment—getting it, refusing it, you name it—requires parental consent. Any directive I write will be worthless without my parents' permission.

"I mean, I can control this," I repeat. "But only if you let me."

Mom still doesn't say anything in response. She just sits there, kneading the muscle on one side of her hand over and over.

"Mom?"

"I heard you, Astrid. I heard you."

Then she gets up and walks away. A minute later, Celia's hand is on my shoulder. She wheels me back inside, but my mother is already gone.

And she doesn't come back, not for the whole rest of the afternoon. I talk to Mohit when he gets out of school, and I avoid the internet like the plague. An orderly brings another tasteless meal of chicken soup and green beans, most of which I leave on the tray. But all the time, I feel myself waiting.

It isn't until I'm pretending to be asleep that I hear the door click open.

She runs her fingers along my bare arm, feeling the warmth of my skin, and puts her cheek against mine. Then she sits down and gently swings her legs onto the bed, so she's resting next to me. She smells like herself. Even after days in this hospital, Mom still smells like home.

53.

I MUST FALL ASLEEP FOR REAL, BECAUSE THEN
I'm awake again, and Mom's gone. It takes me a moment to
register that it's my parents' voices in the hall outside that
woke me up.

"Maybe, just maybe, you should consider giving her what
she wants here," says my father.

"Please, Richard. You have no right to waltz in here and
suddenly start advocating for her ending her life prematurely.
No right."

"That's not what this is, Maxine. It's not. It's giving our
daughter some agency. She's sixteen—she's not a baby. It's
not all our choice."

"It's not *your* choice, that's for sure."

"I'm her father, Maxine. You remember, the other half
who brought her into this world?"

Mom laughs. "And you think biology gives you the right
to take her out of this world against my wishes? She almost

died once before. She came back to us that time. She could still come back to us this time."

There's a pause, and I have to strain to hear if they're still talking.

Eventually Dad's voice comes back. "I'm not advocating for one thing or another here. I'm just saying, this is probably the last choice she gets to make for herself. You're right, okay? I haven't been as much of a parent to her as you have, not in a long time. You've raised her, and you've raised her well. You raised her to be brave. To be clear-eyed. To think for herself. If this is the last choice she gets to make for her life, shouldn't we let her make it?"

They go around and around, until finally my mother breaks down in tears and their voices quiet, and whatever else is said, I can't hear.

54.

A SMALL CONTINGENT OF PEOPLE CALLING themselves reporters gathers outside the hospital, trying to catch a glimpse of my parents going in or out. Celia fills me in, her voice low like she is sharing a secret.

"You're getting pretty famous, love."

"I don't know why anyone cares how I want to die."

Celia wears a crucifix around her neck, a small one with Jesus molded into the gold cross. She runs her hand over it instinctively, as I've seen her do many times now. Then she clucks her tongue as she helps me prop up my pillows. "These people have nothing better to do."

"Do you think it's wrong? Refusing medical treatment?"

"I'm a nurse. It's not my place to judge."

"But what do you *think*?"

"I think . . ." She cocks her head at me quizzically. "Well, I think each of us makes our choices, and I think we make our own peace with our Lord, or with whatever or whomever we believe in. You're very smart. You know what you want."

"Can you tell my mother that?"

Celia winks at me. "Above my pay grade, love. But I'll go outside and tell those reporters where to shove their questions if you want me to."

It hurts to laugh, like stretching a muscle that's started to atrophy.

55.

THEY SEND US TO THE AIRPORT IN AN AMBU-
lance. While the EMTs pack me onto the gurney, Celia comes
by and pats me on the leg.

"Good luck, love."

She slips her hand in mine. It's warm and wrinkled, soft,
the way I remember my grandmother's hands. I feel the cool
of metal against my palm. When she walks away, I open my
fist and see her crucifix there.

I could be offended. I certainly would've been a year ago.
Maybe I should be now. It's not what I believe. But it's her
faith, and somehow, the gift feels like just that—a gift, not a
judgment.

Almost as soon as we're out of the ambulance, we're accosted
by a guy with a digital recorder. "Excuse me, ma'am, can I
ask you for a comment?"

Mom is loading our luggage onto the outdoor belt. She gives him a dirty look but doesn't say anything.

"Ma'am, why are you letting your daughter choose to end medical treatment?"

"Sir," a TSA agent interjects, "I'm going to have to ask you to step away."

The guy persists. "Why are you letting your daughter end her own life?"

"Mom, ignore him," I say through a clamped jaw.

"Ma'am?"

Finally Mom whirls around. "I'm not letting her do any such thing! I'm forcing her to die exactly the way *I* want her to, don't you know that by now? And if you keep harassing us, I'm not going to let *you* have a choice in the manner of your death either!"

The guy smirks and slinks off, and I know immediately that the narrative about Mom is going to shift from just "negligent parent" to "negligent parent with anger management issues."

"Mom." I sigh. "We need to work on this. 'No comment.' Repeat after me: 'No. Comment.'"

"Oh, shut up, Astrid," she snaps back.

She's never snapped at me like that. She's certainly never told me to shut up. She looks as shocked as I am. Then she starts to laugh, and I start to laugh. And finally the TSA agent starts to laugh, probably because she thinks we're unbelievably weird.

"I'm sorry," Mom says through her giggles. "It's not funny.

It's really . . . not funny. But what the *eff*, right?" She spits out the "eff" like she's actually using a curse word, which makes me laugh even harder. "Astrid! You know what I'm saying? Can't they just let us be?"

Her face is flushed and sweaty, and for an instant I'm full of affection for her, even though I feel like we've been at a mother-daughter standstill for days. "Mom, I kind of enjoy this version of you."

She pulls herself together and wipes her eyes. "Well, I'm glad someone does. Let's just get home."

5 6.

TWO DAYS LATER, WE SEE DR. KLEIN SO SHE
can explain what she sees on my most recent scans. I can already guess what she's going to tell us.

My astrocytoma has grown, in spite of the chemo. That's
why my vision has gotten progressively worse, why I can't see
in the periphery anymore. My tumor made of stars is finally
closing in on me. And it's pressing more heavily on my brain
stem now, hence the shooting back pains. Hence the tingling
and numbness in my legs.

"So, Astrid." I know what she's going to say. Most astrocytomas aren't this aggressive. My astrocytoma is like a *Ses-
ame Street* segment I remember from when I was little: *One of
these things is not like the others.* My astrocytoma isn't like the
rest.

"She can still do the clinical trial though, right?" Mom
asks.

I sigh.

"She can, yes. The tumor still hasn't spread beyond the

brain. But . . ." Dr. Klein doesn't finish the thought. "Yes, she can. If that's what you choose."

"It is," Mom says quickly, at the same moment that I say, "It's not."

"There's no rush to make this decision," says Dr. Klein, frowning at us. "Take some time to think about it. We can also consider . . . other options."

"What other options?" Mom asks.

She looks from me to my mother, her eyes heavy. "Palliative options."

Mom's face tightens.

I put a hand on her knee. "Mom, please. Can we go?"

My mother's eyes are already red, but they're dry, like she's cried these particular tears too many times. In her grief, she looks like a different person.

We go home in silence, and I retreat straight to my room. I'm not going to fight with her anymore. She can't force me. What's she going to do, drag me to the hospital for the trial? Hold me down? I'm seething, but the sadness is even more pointed than the anger. I don't want to spend the rest of my life fighting with my mother.

57.

THE NEXT MORNING, MOM POKES HER HEAD in my room and tells me to order dinner for me and Liam tonight. She'll be working late. She doesn't say anything about anything, just tells me to order whatever we want. "And school sent work home. Don't forget about it," she adds. Because keeping up with precalculus is a super-high priority for me right now.

I spend the better part of the day reading about voluntarily refusing to eat and drink. "It's especially important not to take even sips of water," the internet tells me. You can live a long time without food, but not without water. A few days. Maybe ten. You have to make sure they don't put a feeding tube in—that's key. You might feel thirsty at first, but it will subside.

It will all subside.

Around four, Liam comes home. He yells hello from the front hall, and then I hear the television flick on. I wheel myself into the living room because I'm too lazy to walk and find him lying on the couch, channel-surfing.

"Hey. Aren't you supposed to do homework before TV?"

"Homework's done," he says in a monotone.

"You just got home."

"I did it at Kieran's."

"You're sure?"

"Astriiiiiid." He draws my name out in a long, irritated whine. "I'm sure."

"Mmmkay. What do you want to eat?"

He stares at the television, ignoring me.

"Dude, give me something here. Otherwise, I'm picking and we're having sushi."

"Ugh. No way," he says, twisting his face into a scowl.

"You used to like sushi."

Liam mutters something under his breath.

"What was that, dear brother?"

"I said, since when do you know what I like?"

I hold my hands up in surrender. "Okay, okay. Clearly, you're not happy with me. Want to tell me what's going on?"

"Not really."

I go to the television and turn it off, then block it with my body and the wheelchair. Sometimes I feel like every decent conversation I have with my brother requires me to put myself between him and a screen. "Can you talk to me?"

"I was watching that."

"You haven't done your homework yet. I'll bet you one hundred dollars."

He doesn't respond, which tells me I'm right, because otherwise he would definitely take me up on my bet.

"So tell me what's going on, and I'll forget about the homework *and* let you pick dinner and control the remote for the rest of the night. That's a very fair offer."

He frowns at me, then relents. "You're always really sick. And everyone's talking about you at school. And it's annoying."

I start to smile, but quickly stop myself. I can tell he wants to be taken seriously. "You're right. It *is* annoying."

"And you're kind of famous now, and people are saying mean stuff."

"Like what?"

"Like that Mom and Dad are letting you die because they don't care about you."

I roll myself closer to the couch. "I'm sorry, buddy. Those people are wrong, though. It's actually the opposite. Mom and Dad care so much that they'll do anything they can to keep me here. In fact, I wish they didn't want to do so much."

"What do you mean?"

"Well, I've been sick for a while. You know?"

Liam's eyes search my face. Then he nods quietly.

"Right, so Mom and Dad want me to get better. But if I *can't* get better, I think the best thing they can do for me is not to force me to feel even worse than I already do. Does that make sense?"

"Kinda." He looks back at the black screen of the television. "I just don't want you to go anywhere else. Like, don't go on any more road trips. Okay?"

"Okay. No more road trips."

"And I do like sushi."

"See, I knew that."

He takes the menu from me and picks out way more rolls than he can possibly eat. I let him.

5 8 .

WHEN MOM COMES HOME, LIAM IS PASSED
out next to me on the couch. She lifts him gingerly from
under the blanket and carries him to his room. A moment
later, she reappears in front of me.

"You had sushi?"

"Yup."

She yawns. "Any leftovers?"

"Yup."

"Great, I'm starving," she says, going to the kitchen and
opening the fridge. "I didn't eat that whole shift. Just one of
those days. Sometimes everyone decides to have a baby at
once, and it's like—"

"Mom." I cut her off. "We have to talk about the trial.
Please?"

She comes back into the living room and stands over me,
a plate of sushi in one hand. "You have no idea what this is like
for me. Losing you."

Heat flares in my chest. "You have no idea what this is like for *me*, though."

"Astrid." Mom sits down and puts the plate on the coffee table in front of her. She tugs her hair loose from its haphazard workday bun, letting the curls cascade over her shoulders. "Don't be angry at me, my girl. You think I don't know that? But you're my child. I brought you into this world. You're asking me to let you leave it. You can't know just how impossible that is."

"Exactly, Mom. I'm never going to have a child. I'm never going to know what that feels like. Just like I'm never going to see the Pacific Ocean, or ride in a self-driving car, or go to college, or travel abroad, or watch Liam grow up. I'm not going to be able to hold *your* hand when *you're* dying."

"I don't care about that."

"I do, though. I'll miss everything, Mom. I just want control over this one thing."

Mom picks the rice off a piece of spicy tuna roll and eats a few grains, nothing more. She doesn't say anything else.

Eventually, I wheel myself back to my room. Getting out of the chair and into the bed by myself isn't easy. My legs won't do what they're supposed to; they're stubborn, like they've been asleep and now they have that numb, gummy feeling, except I can't wake them up. I get the chair as close to the bed as I possibly can, hold on to the headboard with one hand and my sheets with the other, and try to guide my body onto the mattress.

It doesn't work. I end up on the floor, slouched next to the bed.

"Dammit."

Suddenly, it all comes crashing down over me. The reality of being completely dependent on other people. The reality that this is only going one way, that there's no turning around. Tears come hot and fast; I practically choke on them. I gag on the snot that pours from my nose.

And then, there's my mother. She just appears, like she always seems to when I need her, and scoops me into her arms and rocks me like I'm someone's newborn baby she's just welcomed into the world. Or like I'm still her newborn, the one she brought into this world herself.

"My girl. My sweet, brave, stubborn girl. Okay." She holds me tighter still. "Okay. I hear you."

59.

ON SUNDAY, MO FINALLY HAS A DAY OFF
from rehearsal. It's not that cold for early March, and he
pushes me outside, just as far as the little grassy patch on the
corner of my block. We sit bundled in the midday sun, watching the cars.

"I wish we could go up the monument," I say.

He nods. "We've seen that view, though. So many times."

60.

CHLOE TEXTS ME IN THE AFTERNOON AND
tells me to check the vlog channel. I dread looking at the page.
I don't want to know anymore how many people have clicked
and shared and liked. I'm tired of Google alerts pinging me
when there's another misleading internet story about me. I'm
tired of being a person other people care about.

I check it anyway, though, because Chloe says so, and I'm
surprised to find a new video. We haven't filmed anything
else, so I have no idea what this is. On-screen, Chloe steps in
front of the camera and then leans in to adjust the focus.

*Hi, everyone. Thanks so much for watching Astrid's videos, for
sending your best wishes, and for making donations. I'm Chloe.
I've been taking the videos. Astrid and I have been best friends
since, like, forever. I mean, it sounds cheesy, but she's the closest thing I have to a sister.*

She pauses there. Her eyes shimmer.

Anyway, many of you watched Astrid's most recent video, and a lot of people seem to have very strong opinions about her decision not to pursue cryopreservation, and to discontinue treatment for cancer and undergo palliative care. I mean, um, we who love her have strong opinions about that, too. Because, you know, we love her. Like in real life. But a lot of you seem to think you know better than Astrid does about what might be the best choice for her. So we thought—well, I thought—you should hear from someone else who has a point of view on this. Before you judge her, or any of us.

The camera cuts out, then starts up again. It takes me a minute before I realize that we're now in my own kitchen. My mother sits by the window, holding her own camera awkwardly at arm's length. It's late, and her face is lit only by the too-bright overhead.

Hello, everyone. I'm Astrid's mother. I'm not very camera-ready, sorry. I'm just going to . . . do my best here to tell you what's going on. Astrid had a seizure while she was on her way back from Arizona. She was hospitalized there, in a medically induced coma for three days, and as soon as she was awake and strong enough, we transported her home. Her tumor has grown, but . . .

She looks away, then back at the camera.

We're hoping for the best, still. She's a fighter.

Pause.

And I want to thank you all for . . . caring. Even if you disagree with what Astrid wants to do now.

Pause.

I was . . . uncertain about all of this. I was uncertain about Astrid's original idea to pursue cryopreservation. About the idea of videoing the whole thing and asking strangers for money. I didn't like that very much at all. And now, certainly, about her decision to discontinue treatment—well, you can imagine. I'm her mother. I'm not as . . . I wasn't willing to see that we might not be able to cure this, to accept that Astrid might want to seek out alternative possibilities for how to live the rest of her life. And for her death. I thought she could just fight, and then she'd win.

Her voice falters briefly, but she holds herself together.

The truth is, that's not fair to her. She's only human. She's doing her best. If there is no cure for Astrid, that's on us, not her.

My face burns. Mom laughs uncomfortably.

Astrid loves science. She always has. When she was little, she used to mix different things together in our kitchen—you know, seltzer water, baking soda, food coloring, whatever she could find—to see what would happen. She became interested in the brain in particular after she first got sick, two years ago, and I think she would make a great neuroscientist one day. She loves life. But she also wants to die on her terms. And I . . .

A tear rolls down my mother's cheek, but she ignores it.

I can't say now—after sixteen years of raising my daughter to be an independent thinker—I can't say, "You have to live and die on my terms, not yours." So I'm ready to support whatever choices she makes for the rest of her life, however long that might be. Whatever those choices are, they'll be the right ones for her. I want to thank those of you who have supported her journey. And for those of you who think you'd know better how to handle this, well, I hope you never have to find out how wrong you are. Okay, that's it. I'm finished. Thanks.

The video cuts out.
I didn't feel myself starting to cry, but my face is wet.

61.

Dear Dr. Fitzspelt,

Thank you again for hosting us in February, and for the tour. I wanted to let you know that I have decided not to pursue cryopreservation after my death. This might sound weird, but I also want to thank you for helping me come to that decision. Not because your program wasn't compelling, but because you helped me understand what I wanted from the end of my life. I want to write the story myself, as you said. I've found a better way to do that.

I hope you do find a way to revive your clients one day. I have faith that you will.

All my best,
Astrid

62.

MOHIT'S SHOW AT THE REGATTABAR IS ON A
Wednesday in the beginning of April. Mom takes me shopping at T.J.Maxx for a "special-occasion dress," as she calls it,
although I'm not convinced that you're supposed to wear a
dress to a jazz club. I sort of imagined wearing black jeans and
a black T-shirt and maybe dark sunglasses, but Mom doesn't
seem to agree with my vision. As she flips through the rack of
"Off the Runway" dresses, tagged in purple with their dis-
counted prices, she slings possibilities over the crook of her
arm: there's a royal-blue silk with an asymmetrical hem, a red
halter, something with pink tulle.

"Mom, no. I would never wear any of those."

She rolls her eyes and keeps digging. Then my hand grazes
soft black lace. When I pull it out from the rack, I know it's
the one, even without trying it on. The dress is stretchy, with
long sleeves but a short skirt, like a long, fitted shirt. It'll
cover up the now-defunct chemo port on my chest and the IV

scars on my arms but show off my legs, which still look normal even if they don't work the way they used to.

"That's it," Mom says, nodding. "That's the one."

I check the purple tag. It's pricey, even at its steep discount. Mom puts her hand over mine and grabs the dress.

"It doesn't matter," she says. "We're not looking at price tags today."

In the dressing room, Mom helps me pull the lace over my sunken chest and bony rib cage, and because it's so stretchy, I'm not even swimming in it. It just encases my body, what's left of it. I run my hands over the soft fuzz that's grown back across my scalp and smile in the mirror. Lately, all I've seen when I look at myself is what isn't there anymore: the flesh and muscle, the color in my cheeks, the energy I used to have. But right now I look just like myself.

At the checkout counter, the woman behind the cash register eyes both of us. My story faded easily from the public's interest, gone as quickly as it came, but we still occasionally get looks of recognition. I see the moment in the cashier's face when she remembers why we look familiar.

"Yes, it's us," I say. "The kid who wants to die and the mother who's willing to let her."

"Astrid," Mom whispers.

The cashier looks mortified. She doesn't say anything, just slips the dress into a plastic bag.

"We don't need the receipt," says Mom. "The dress isn't coming back."

As we make our way toward the automatic doors, the woman calls after us. "God bless you both!"

Outside, in the cold of early spring, Mom and I take one look at each other and burst into a fit of giggles.

The Regattabar is not the smoky jazz club I'd always imagined, probably because smoking indoors in public places is now illegal in Massachusetts, which is just as well, because lung cancer isn't high on my list of must-haves. But it is warm and hazy, with low light and tables facing a small stage with a parquet floor. Mo had to be here early, so I came with his parents.

"You all right, dear?" Mr. Parikh lets me lean heavily on his arm to get to the front of the club. He looks me over with concern as he settles me at a table.

"I'm good, thanks. Where'd Mrs. Parikh go? Want to sit?" There are two more empty seats at my table, but he shakes his head.

"We'll take our own table. I promised Mohit we wouldn't sit right in the front." He chuckles.

"Oops. Well, I made no such promises."

"I think you can get away with whatever you want."

I order a Coke from a waitress, and Mr. Parikh tells her to add it to his bill.

★

When Mo sees me, it's almost like he's seeing me for the first time. His face jolts like he's just had an electrical shock, then slides into a smile.

His group is just the opener for some bigger and fancier jazz ensemble that isn't composed of three college nerds and a high schooler, but it doesn't matter. I already know, as soon as Mohit puts the saxophone to his lips, that I won't remember the real act anyway. When he plays, it's just how I thought it would be: like floating on a calm ocean with the sun on my skin and no one else in sight except the two of us.

I close my eyes and pretend we're already living in the future I'll never see, the one where we're grown-up and he's a musician and I'm a scientist and we live in New York City and he headlines at the jazz clubs and I sit in the front and drink fancy cocktails. I know each tune before he plays it, even the ones he improvises. Every note is perfect.

The apartment is dark when Mohit wheels me inside. I can see Mom's light on under her door, but everything is still and quiet.

"You were pretty great tonight," I tell Mo one more time, even though I've been gushing all the way home.

"Thanks. It was pretty great to have you there."

"Sorry I sat right in the front."

"You can get away with it on account of that dress."

I swat his arm lightly. "Oh, I see. So all you care about is how I look, huh? How enlightened-twenty-first-century male of you."

"Yeah, yeah. Whatever. You can get away with anything because of how intelligent and humorous and persistent and kind-hearted you are. Better?"

I nod.

He kisses me, then grins. "And also because of that dress."

Then he kisses me again. I tell him to carry me to my bedroom, and he does, and shuts the door behind us.

63.

MOM DECLARES THE NEXT DAY A SUNDAY,
even though it's actually a Thursday. It's her day off, and she
tells Liam he's playing hooky, too. He practically levitates,
he's so excited. Mom makes pancakes and we hole up on the
couch, watching a marathon of *The Great British Baking Show* on
Netflix.

"My kiddos," Mom says, settling herself between the two
of us. Liam snuggles in under the throw that's draped over
our laps. "I did pretty good with you two, I must admit."

"Not bad," I concur. "Could be worse."

On the show, a cab driver with a deep scar on his temple
is making a 3-D pirate-ship scene out of chocolate cookies and
marshmallow fondant. He leans over his pastel workstation
with a piping bag squeezed between both hands, his face ob-
scured as he paints the most precise patterns on the edges of
his pirate ships.

"This guy's going to win!" Liam shouts. "Look at that.
That's awesome."

"No, he messed up his technical challenge. The girl with the round glasses is going to win."

My phone vibrates in my pocket. A text from Chloe.

Did you see? Your guy died.

What guy??? I write back quickly.

Your rock climber.

I open Google and type "free solo death" into the browser. Sure enough, several recent news items pop up. I click the first one, an article from *Outside* online.

Aidan Wallace, 27, the young climber who made a name for himself—and history—free soloing some of the toughest big walls in the nation, died yesterday after a fall from Bell Rock in Sedona, Arizona.

Wallace, who is perhaps best known for completing the only known free solo of the Yosemite Triple Crown, was out for a casual day of climbing, according to his girlfriend, Yesenia Ortiz. "Bell Rock was an easy climb for him. It was nothing. It was like a warm-up," Ortiz said.

But without a rope of any kind—completely free on the wall, his preferred style of climbing—even a warm-up can end in tragedy.

"I was waiting for him at the top," Ortiz said. "I didn't hear or see him come off the wall. I'm not sure what

happened. But I do know he died doing what he
loved most in this world, which was being alone on
the wall, with nothing between him and the sky."

Bell Rock. I look it up to be sure, but I already know I'm
right. Bell Rock is one of the two red rock formations Mohit
and I stared at from the top of Eagle's Nest. That view, the
one that burned itself into my memory. We could've seen
Aidan Wallace climbing there.

I should be sad for him, or at least for his family. He was
only twenty-seven. He'll never climb again, never kiss his
girlfriend, who seems perfectly nice. He won't marry her or
become a dad. He'll miss everything. I should be sad. But I'm
not. Because Yesenia Ortiz is right. He had the perfect kind
of death. And even though I'm sure he didn't *choose* it in the
sense of coming off that wall on purpose, he *did* choose to
live—and leave—on his own terms. Wherever he is, I'm sure
he has no regrets.

64.

LIKE I KNOW THEY WILL, THE SEIZURES COME
back.

First, a small one.

Then another, longer.

65.

ON A TUESDAY NIGHT IN MAY, CHLOE SITS BY
my bed, not talking, just reading on her phone. It's like any
other night, except this one happens to be a Tuesday.

"What are you reading?"

"Nothing." She sighs.

"What?"

"Nothing, I just . . . It's late."

I have no idea what time it is. "Okay."

"I have to be up early tomorrow. I'm at Mom A's tonight."

"Can you just stay a little while longer?" I roll my head
toward the edge of the pillow and try to give her Sad Eyes so
she'll stay. Maybe I'm being a pain in the ass, but Mom's at
work and Liam's sleeping at Kieran's. I like the feeling of having someone here. I remember when I used to wish for quiet.
Now an empty apartment feels too big.

She sighs. "Astrid, it takes forever to get to her new place.
If you'd ever come over, you would know that."

"Clo—"

"I have a life, Astrid. I'm sorry you don't, but I do."

Then she's gone.

She doesn't come back the next day, or answer her phone.

66.

I'M NOT SURE IF IT'S THE DAY AFTER, OR THE
day after that, they blur together.

"I brought you soft serve." Chloe drops her bag in the corner and installs herself next to my bed. She unpacks a Styro-
foam cup of ice cream from an insulated paper bag and pops
the to-go cover off the top. Chocolate with chocolate sprinkles. "Also, sorry I was a jerk the other night."

"I'm sorry I haven't come over to your new place yet."
Yet. As though there will be a time when I will visit Annalisa's new apartment and help Chloe decorate her room. We
both know there won't be. But we let it go.

67.

I TURN SEVENTEEN.

Liam blows out my candles.
I let him take the wish.

68.

ON MY RIGHT SIDE, I LOSE MOST OF THE FEELING in my arm and leg, like I've had a stroke. Like I'm old. I feel old.

My mother helps me to the bathroom.

Chloe helps me to the bathroom.

Mohit helps me to the bathroom.

"I don't want you to," I say to Mo. I'm whimpering—even though I want to be strong, and strong people don't whimper.

The bathroom is too small. He turns his back while I pee to give me the illusion of privacy, but it doesn't work. I close my eyes, try to pretend I'm alone, functional, normal.

I can still wipe myself. At least there's that. I'll keep eating and drinking as long as I don't need a catheter.

Mo pulls my pants up over my knees. "Why not? I don't care."

"I don't want you to remember me smelling like pee."

"You don't smell like pee."

"Right."

Things I'll miss when I'm dead (a partial list, continued):

The smell of the radiators giving off steam heat in the winter

The smell of fresh air circulating in the house in the spring

The smell of sunscreen and Liam's sweat in the summer

The smell of leaves and end-of-the-season grilling in fall

Human touch

Netflix

Being loved

70.

DAD AND SUZANNE COME, WITH THE BABY.
Alice Turner-Ayeroff. She's bigger now, almost three months
old, much more human-like than she was in that first picture.

They bring her to my room and lay her on the bed with
me. I put my palm to her cheek and she makes a gurgling
noise.

71.

I HAVE ANOTHER SEIZURE, A LONGER ONE.

Then another, longer still.

I sleep most of the time, for days.

I hear Dr. Klein's voice. She's in our apartment, and my parents are out in the hall, talking with her.

When she comes back in the room, Mom's cheeks are streaked with red.

I'm sorry.

I'm sorry, Mom. I shouldn't do this to you.

72.

THE AIR WARMS, JUST A LITTLE, AND MOHIT drives me to the Bunker Hill Monument. He wheels me to the base, and we stare up at it in silence. It's familiar, the way the obelisk cuts the sky. Our view.

73.

WE WATCH MOVIES.

We order pizza. I can barely taste the bite I put on my tongue, but I eat it anyway.

Liam watches me tentatively, all the time. He doesn't ask questions, just watches.

Some classmates send cards home and Chloe reads them out loud, rolling her eyes at the girls who claim to "love me so much" when we've barely spoken since freshman year.

74.

MOM TAKES LIAM TO THE MUSEUM OF SCIENCE

for a whole afternoon to "give him a break." Mohit stays with me, tucked into the bed next to me.

"Take your clothes off," I tell him. He does, then mine, also at my request. Our bodies are warm next to each other. He touches every inch of my scarred, pathetic flesh with the gentlest fingertips.

It sends tingles, the good kind, through my spine.

My body is still capable of pleasure.

My body is not capable of many things, but there is still pleasure.

75.

AND THEN THERE ISN'T.

Cancer can break your bones, did you know that? I didn't. It can. My spine fractures under the weight of my own cells.

The days are shorter.

They're not, really. Still twenty-four hours in each.

Shorter for me.

76.

HOSPICE SENDS NURSES. USUALLY IT'S ONE
named Nell, except when she's off, and then it's someone else.
I like Nell. She doesn't try to make too much conversation.
She's not Celia, though.

The pain meds feel good, but they make me sleepy. When
I need them, I can press a button that sends a fresh dose into
my bloodstream.

I try to play a game with myself: *Don't Press That Button*.

I always lose.

77.

I DECIDE TO DRINK MY LAST SIP OF WATER ON
one of these summer Sundays. It's July and there's a heat wave.
Everyone who comes into my room is sweating and complain-
ing.

I'm cold.

When I dehydrate, I'll gradually lose consciousness. I
won't feel any pain. Then I'll just drift off, and that'll be it.

"Why a Sunday?" Mo asks. He keeps asking if they should
put the air conditioner in my window because it's so hot in
the room. Mom has to remind him, again, that it's not necessary. I'm not hot.

And when I'm gone, it'll be a waste of electricity.

"Why not a Sunday?" I say. "Day of rest and all that."

He rolls his eyes.

"Hey." I shove him. "You hate it when I do that."

Those eyes fill.

78.

MY BRAIN IS BROKEN. BUT MY MIND?

My mind is all mine. Strong enough still to make my own choices.

79.

IT'S THE MIDDLE OF THE NIGHT, BUT I CALL MO
anyway. He sounds anxious when he answers the phone.

"I thought I was afraid of missing everything," I tell him.

"I know." He's groggy.

"But I'm not anymore. I'm just afraid the things I'll miss
won't happen."

"I don't know what you mean."

"Promise you'll always play music? If you don't, I won't
miss it. But I don't want you to ever stop."

"Okay. I'll always play music."

"And you'll go bald and get married and have kids?"

"I mean, probably. Maybe not the bald part."

"Your dad is bald, though. You'll probably go bald."

"Thanks, Astrid." He sighs. "I love you."

"And I love you."

"So we agree on that. Can we go to sleep now and I'll see
you tomorrow?"

"Remember our Venn diagram?" I ask.

"Our what?"

"Faith in your circle, science in mine. Architects in the overlapping middle. The possible Venn diagram of our belief systems."

"Why architects?"

"I don't know. Because you have to know physics to make buildings stand up? And you also have to have faith?"

I can hear him smiling, even through his half sleep. "Okay. Good night, Astrid."

"Good night, Mo."

I hang up. I press the button for more pain medication. While I wait for it to seep into my system, I close my eyes and watch bits of light dance behind my eyelids. They look like the Perseids, pieces of burning comet debris rocketing through the night sky. Or shooting stars.

My tumor made of stars.

The view from here is beautiful.